Canned

By

Lynda L. Lock

&

your Friend Sparky

Dedication

In loving memory of my best friend and adventure partner, Lawrie Lock. We crammed a lot of escapades into 39 years of love, laughter, and dancing. Lots of dancing.

Prologue

Christmas Eve, Kelowna airport

Stepping off the plane in Kelowna on Christmas Eve, Jessica Sanderson stuffed her rebellious blonde hair under her light jacket and zipped it up. It was the downside to traveling between Mexico and Canada in December. Her jacket was never perfect. It was like the three bears and their porridge. The jacket was too hot when she arrived in Cancun, and too cold when she landed in Kelowna. She seldom got it just right.

Her nine-day visit with her Isla Mujeres friends had passed quickly. She was looking forward to reuniting with her partner Mike Lyons, and her Mexi-mutt, Sparky, in time for their Christmas celebrations. But, damn she was cold. As one island friend said, there was no good reason to be in Canada in the winter, except for love.

And she loved Mike. Unconditionally. So here she was, in Canada, in the winter.

Mike, a respected winemaker who traveled extensively as a freelance consultant, currently had two Okanagan projects on the go; *No Regrets*, located between Penticton and Okanagan Falls, and *On the Edge*, overlooking the Village of Naramata. Perched high above the lakeshore, *On the Edge Winery* is located a bit north of the village of

Naramata on a narrow country road that twists past a collection of vineyards and orchards.

Following a family tragedy, the owners Dr. Keegan and Danielle Crawford, offered Mike and Jessica the guest cottage, rent-free, for as long as Mike worked for their winery.

Jessica worked at both wineries wherever another pair of hands was needed, picking grapes, pruning vines, bottling the wines, or occasionally helping out in the wine shops. It was a good life, in a beautiful part of the world, but the sweeping vineyards, sparkling lakes, and fruit-laden orchards still took a back seat to her previous life on the Caribbean coast of Mexico.

Walking carefully to minimize the pressure on her broken middle toe, a memento from her visit to Mexico, she pulled her small suitcase along the featureless and chilly jetway, heading toward CBSA, the Canada Border Services Agency. With nothing to declare, she was swiftly processed and proceeded to the main terminal. Her eyes scanned left and right searching for Mike.

"Jess!"

"Mike," she shouted back, waving excitedly. A few more feet and she stepped into his embrace and kissed him passionately. "Merry Christmas Eve, my love," she pulled back a little to see his wide, warm smile. "Damn, I've missed you."

"Welcome home and a very Merry Christmas to you. Sparky and I have missed you too."

"Did Sparky come with you?"

"Yes, he's outside. Unhappy at being left in the car," he said, reaching for the handle of her small carry-on suitcase. "Is this all you have?"

Gripping his free hand, she matched his stride as they headed to the exit. "Yes, just the one suitcase that I left with. I didn't buy anything while I was away." She stepped outside and gasped. "Shit! That's cold."

"Yep, it's minus twenty-six tonight." Mike lifted her suitcase to avoid dragging it through the mess of ice melter and dirty snow.

"It was lovely and warm when I boarded the plane in Cancun," Jessica sighed, "I miss the weather almost as much as I miss my friends," she said, eyeing Mike, "I hope you drove up here in one of the winery vehicles. Your old MGTC convertible doesn't do winter."

"The MGTC is not old, it's a desirable classic car," Mike rebutted, then pointed a remote control at a new, turquoise-blue Jeep Wrangler. "The MGTC might not do winter, but that certainly does," he said, as the engine started.

"Cool color. Who does it belong to?"

"It's ours. Sparky and I went car shopping while you were away," he said. "I sold the convertible to a collector in California, and bought this."

"Hot damn!" she said. "Okay, I'm a little bit sorry you sold your toy," she said, holding her forefinger and thumb a tiny distance apart, "but it will be so nice to have a regular vehicle with proper windows, a heater, and A/C for the summer."

Mike had bought the 1948 sports car a few months back because he wanted to learn how to drive a right-hand drive, a British vehicle. The nearly seventy-year-old car was bare-bones basic compared to modern-day cars. A wrench was required to adjust the seats. The floor gearshift was on the British side, the left side of the driver. The low-slung car couldn't be used in deep snow. The heater was inadequate. And the side windows snapped into place. With a happy grin on his face, he told Jessica he had bought it as a present for her. She'd thanked, mentally rolled her eyes, and planned to buy something more suitable as soon as she returned from her trip to Mexico. She could now cross that item off her to-do list.

"It even has heated seats, for you milady." He said opening the passenger door to a wiggling blur of black and white fur.

"Sparky baby, I've missed you." She scooped his stocky body into her arms and tried to kiss his snout while her normally calm and quiet dog squirmed and whined excitedly.

"He thought you had abandoned him forever," Mike said as he popped her suitcase in the back, and got into the driver's side. "All set?"

"Just a minute," she said, setting Sparky on the seat. "Come on Sparky. Move over and let me in." Hoisting her backside onto the seat, she removed her gloves and fastened her seatbelt. "Good to go."

Mike quietly stared at her, "When were you going to tell me about your banged-up hands?" he asked, nodding at the healing scars.

Surprised that he had noticed, she looked at her ungloved hands. "I'm really tired. Can I tell you on the way home?"

"The real story or an abridged version?"

"I'll give you the basics, and we can discuss my trip tomorrow morning while we drink coffee by the fire and open our Christmas gifts. Deal?"

"Was I supposed to buy you a Christmas gift?" he asked putting the vehicle in drive.

"Damn straight! And it had better be a fabulous gift."

"Hmm. That could be a problem. But I can offer you a breakfast mimosa instead of coffee."

"Coffee first. I need my morning jolt of caffeine. Then a mimosa and presents. Fabulous presents. A pile of presents," she teased.

"Do you think the 7-Eleven is still open? They usually have stuff for last-minute gifts," he said, tapping the tip of his index finger against his lips. He looked thoughtful for a moment. "I've got a better idea. I'll decorate the Jeep with a big red bow, and put the keys in a gift-wrapped box under the tree. But you have to promise to be surprised," he said straight-faced.

Jessica grinned at his profile. *Was he serious? At least a toasty warm Jeep was a better present than a 1948 classic car.*

Chapter 1

Cactus Brewing

Smooth concrete floors, moody dark grey walls, and thick wooden timbers gave the brewery an industrial feel, and yet the interior of the taproom felt cozy and inviting. The bar was made from polished concrete and stainless steel. Enormous, changeable chalkboards hung on the back wall above the bar, listing the current offerings for food, local wines, and the brewery's offering of ales and lagers.

Pretending to be occupied with wiping the tabletops, Olivia Caponera whispered to her co-worker, "I can't wait for tonight."

"It's going to be epic," Hayley VanBeck agreed. "We should take a taxi so we can enjoy ourselves."

"I don't have any money," Olivia said. Almost two years ago, she'd been hired to work in the taproom, yet she was always broke. During the busy summer months when the tips were plentiful, she spent her money on anything she wanted. By the September long weekend, her hours were dramatically reduced as the business slowed in the months leading up to Christmas. She hadn't saved anything. As much as she hated living at home, it wasn't a terrible set-up. No rent. No utilities. Free meals and internet. Bearable. If her mother and her mother's second husband didn't crowd her.

Suddenly Olivia had a thought and she grinned slyly at Hayley.

"What are you thinking?" Hayley asked.

"Sarah has a car." Dropping the menus on the counter, Olivia strutted toward the younger new hire. "Hey Sarah, do you want to hang out with Hayley and me?"

"Really?" Sarah asked. She stopped restocking the serving stations and smiled hopefully at Olivia. "I'd love to." Olivia and Hayley had been the brightest stars of the in-crowd at high school, while she had been exiled to the dark, outer edge of their universe. This was the first time, ever, that Olivia had said anything more to her than a grunted demand to fetch restaurant supplies.

"We've been invited to an amazing party tonight. You just have to come with us," Olivia gushed. "It's going to be on fire."

"Oh, tonight? Then I can't go. It's Christmas Eve, and I'm spending it with my family," Sarah said, her face drooping with disappointment.

"We're not going until later. You'll have lots of time to spend with your mommy and daddy," Olivia taunted. "Then later you can be a grownup and go out with us."

Sarah blushed. "I don't think I should. My family values our Christmas Eve traditions. But thank you so much for the invite. I appreciate your thoughtfulness."

Switching tactics, Olivia said, "Tell your mom that you are going out for an hour with a couple of friends. For God's sake Sarah, you're old enough to make your own rules."

Sarah looked down at her feet, wishing Olivia would just take no for an answer, "Really, I can't." She had just started working at the brewery, and she didn't want to lose the chance to be friends with Olivia. Unlike her kitchen workmates who included her in their gentle teasing and companionship, Olivia and Hayley, had until this moment ignored her.

"Well, I am surprised. I thought you were one of us. Someone cool to hang out with. Someone that we could be good friends with. I guess I made a big mistake," she said over one shoulder as she walked away.

"Wait."

With her back to Sarah, Olivia smiled to herself. *Gotcha.*

"Okay, I'll go. Just for an hour. Where should I meet you?"

"Wow that's great," Olivia retraced her steps and enthusiastically enfolded Sarah in a hug. "That's fabulous. Let's all go together. You've got a car, so pick us up at eleven at my house. I'll text you my address," Olivia chattered, not allowing Sarah to object. "What's your phone number?"

"Um, okay," Sarah said, supplying her phone number, "but, only for an hour."

"Yeah, yeah. I got it," she walked toward Hayley, holding her hand close to her chest she gave Hayley a thumbs up.

"What did she say?" Hayley whispered.

"The nerd is going to drive us," Olivia said. "I told her to pick us up at my house at eleven."

"Okay, I'll get Dad to drop me off," Hayley said. Her family lived in a modest neighborhood, a distance from where Olivia's wealthier parents owned a large, modern home.

"Does he know that we are going out?" Olivia asked.

"No, I said that I was going to watch movies with you because your parents were out, and you didn't want to be alone on Christmas Eve," Hayley said sheepishly.

"Yeah, that's fine. Stephanie and Kent won't be home until later," she said referring to her mother and her mother's second husband by their first names. "And they don't check to see if I am home or not. We have a mature relationship," she added, implying that she was more grown up than Hayley.

"Does Sarah have a curfew?" Hayley asked.

"She says she can only stay for an hour, but we'll see about that."

"If she doesn't want to stay, we can share a taxi home," Hayley replied.

"I told you. I don't have any money."

Puzzled, Hayley didn't argue. Olivia's parents were rich. Really rich. "Well, if we get stuck, I have money."

"Don't worry. I've got it under control. She is dying to be my bestie."

Chapter 2

Condo complex

"Hey, Lucas. We're here. Buzz us in!" A female voice said.

"Who's us?"

"Olivia and Hayley," she replied, then added, "and Sarah. Open up! We're freezing to death."

"Okay," Lucas Bankole replied, as he used his phone to unlock the main entrance and activate the elevator. He turned to his roommate, Connor. "Two hot chicks, and one unknown."

Bankole was known as Lucas to the young women, Louis to the people living in the complex, and simply LB to those who knew him a little better, like his most recent roommate, Connor. His father, a tough, abusive bastard, had called him another name: a fricking waste of prime sperm. Thankfully the son of a bitch had died last year, and he was once again able to visit his mother whenever he was in Toronto.

Lucas unlocked the door and propped his long, toned body against the kitchen counter, waiting for the girls.

"We're here. Where's the party?" Olivia said, flinging the door with enough force to bounce it against the doorstop.

"I thought you said there were three of you?" Lucas crossed his arms and stared at the slightly built young man who hovered timidly behind the three girls.

"This is Noah. He works with us. He's cool," Olivia said, dismissively.

"Hi," Noah bounced his head in a nervous nod.

"Hi yourself," Lucas said. He didn't appreciate Olivia surprising him with this guy. He would allow it, this time. Wrapping his arms around her, he gripped her tightly and pulled her body against his groin while kissing her. Breaking the kiss, he turned his head slightly and said to Connor, "This is Olivia." Then he pointed at the other young women. "I know you're Hayley, so you must be Sarah."

They nodded, yes.

"And who are you?" Hayley asked Connor. Her lips tweaked in a lazy smile as her eyes explored his body.

"Connor."

"Connor what?"

"Just Connor."

"Okay then, *Just* Connor, do you want to party with me?" Hayley leaned in and while looking into his eyes she lightly ran her fingernail down his arm, imitating a sexy move that she'd seen in a movie.

Surprised, Connor raised an eyebrow and flicked a look at Noah to see if he had other ideas about who was going to party with Hayley. Noah looked away. No backbone. "What have you got in mind?" Connor asked her.

"A little private time, one on one," Hayley winked, hoping she looked enticing.

"Let's get this party started with a little hit of something fun," Olivia said, loudly, blocking out Connor's keen agreement to Hayley's suggestion.

"Help yourself to the gummies on the coffee table," Lucas said.

"Gummies?" Olivia asked. "Where are you hiding the good shit?"

"Just wait a minute, Olivia. What about you Sarah?" Lucas asked the plump brunette lingering near the entrance.

"Nothing for me thanks," she held up a hand, waving off a suggestion that she should sample the drugs. "I'm the designated driver tonight."

Hayley rolled her eyes. "Don't be a baby. Come on, try something."

"No, really, I'm fine," Sarah's eyebrows pinched together as she shook her mousey brown hair. *This is a really stupid idea*. She thought. She wished she had held her ground and stayed home to celebrate Christmas Eve with her family. Olivia hadn't said anything about taking drugs or partying with older guys. She'd said she wanted to drop in on some friends and wish them Merry Christmas. "Don't forget, Livy, I told Mom I'd be back in an hour or two," she said.

Noticing Olivia's annoyed expression, Lucas winked at her but spoke to Sarah. "Don't worry, Sarah, I'll make sure you aren't late."

Hayley waved her arms over her head. "Then let's get this party started!"

"Hey, man. You got a minute?" Connor asked Lucas, pointing toward his bedroom.

"Sure," Lucas followed his roommate and shut the door. "What's up?"

"I'm all for having a good time, but are these chicks legal age?" Connor asked.

Lucas shrugged. "Before you moved in, Olivia and Hayley were regular visitors. They are older than they look. Plus, I've made it very clear what would happen if they talk about me, or any of my friends."

"What about Sarah? She looks terrified. Like she was forced to come here."

"I'll make her a special drink and calm her down a bit. She'll be fine," Lucas said. He opened the bedroom door and headed to the kitchen.

"My special Christmas Eve drinks for everyone, coming up," Lucas said, as he turned his back on the group and crushed two Ativan tablets into the drink intended for Sarah. He stirred, blending the white powder into the fruity concoction of cranberry, grapefruit juice, and vodka. Putting the six drinks on a tray, he made a show of playing the host. He handed a glass to each person, ensuring that Sarah got the drink intended for her. Holding up his drink, he said, "Merry Christmas everyone. Drink up!" He tipped his glass, watching her.

Sarah sipped, then started to set the glass on a table, when Olivia said. "Come on Sarah. It's only one drink and it's mostly juice."

"It's true Sarah, it's almost all cranberry and grapefruit juices," Lucas assured the timid girl.

She reluctantly put the glass to her lips and drank deeply.

"See, what did I tell you? It's a very weak drink," he said.

Sarah quietly sat in one corner of the long black couch, cradling the glass in her hand. She glanced around, looking for something to comment on, to pretend she was interested in being here in the apartment of two strangers. From where she sat in the living room, she could see a massive television mounted above the gas fireplace, two expensive e-bikes, a bright yellow kayak, and a pile of gaming paraphernalia. A glimpse into one of the bedrooms revealed another enormous television hanging on the wall, and piles of clothing. They had a lot of belongings for two guys living on their own, but maybe that was because they were older. Late twenties?

The one named Lucas could even be over thirty, she wasn't sure. His lean body and dark skin made it harder to guess his age. Connor had a sturdier body, with curly blonde hair and pale freckled skin. He looked younger than Lucas and close to ten years older than her.

She trembled slightly, wishing she hadn't let Hayley and Olivia intimidate her into being their driver. She wasn't completely naïve. She knew they invited her because she owned a car. Her old Hyundai was functional, and owning it had increased her social status with her trendy workmates. And then at the last minute, they had included Noah in the group. Olivia had claimed Lucas, and Hayley had claimed Connor, and it appeared that they expected her to keep Noah company. She barely knew him, other than he worked at Cactus Brewing with Olivia, Hayley, and herself. *Why did I let myself get talked into this? It's Christmas Eve, and I should be at home. I could pretend there is a family emergency, and I have to leave immediately.*

She grabbed her phone, starting a text to her mom...*please call me. I need...*

"Sarah, are you ready for another drink?" Lucas asked.

Worried he might see the message to her mom, she quickly turned her phone over and looked up at Lucas, "I still have some left, thank you."

"Tip it up girl, it doesn't taste good when it gets warm," he said.

Reluctantly she drained the glass and set it in his outstretched hand. "Thank you. That was refreshing," she said. In truth, the last mouthful had an oddly bitter taste.

"Are you sure I can't interest you in another?"

"No, thank you. Maybe later," she put a hand to her forehead and blinked several times.

"Sure. Just let me know," he turned and saw Olivia watching Sarah. He lightly touched her arm, warning her not to say anything. She looked up and gave him a discreet nod.

Then Lucas reached into a cupboard and set a bowl containing capsules of several different prescription and street drugs on the counter. "Help yourself."

Hayley grabbed the bowl and poked through the contents, then popped a capsule in her mouth. She stroked Connor's arm. "Now, how about that private party?"

Noah watched Hayley, then picked up the same type of capsule, "Is this the good stuff?"

"I guess we'll find out," she replied. Her eyes never left Connor's face.

Connor pointed at his bedroom. "Lead the way, Hayley." He glanced at Lucas and tipped his head toward Sarah as she covered a yawn.

Lucas nodded, and retrieved a pillow from his bedroom, "Sarah, you look tired. Why don't you have a little nap?" He said, placing the pillow on the couch, and gently pushing on her left shoulder to encourage her to stretch out.

"What? No. I'm fine," she rigidly braced her right arm to hold herself upright.

"No, you're not. Have a nap. We'll be in the bedroom if you need anything."

"I 'ave to go. It's Christmas Eve, and I promised my mom," she mumbled and slumped sideways.

Lucas slid his hands under her and shifted her body so that her feet would also be on the sofa.

"Wha' you doin?" she asked. "Call Mom. Need her."

"You're fine, I'm just making sure you don't fall on the floor."

"kay," she mumbled.

Lucas watched her for a moment. Her breathing slowed down as she drifted into a deep sleep. "She's asleep."

"Jesus, Lucas, I thought you were going to relax her, not knock her out," Olivia said.

"I misjudged her tolerance. She'll be fine," he leveled a look at Noah. "Keep an eye on her. We're going to be busy for a bit," he said, scooping up several capsules and ushering Olivia into his bedroom.

Noah stood in the middle of the living room. Both bedroom doors were tightly shut, excluding him, and Sarah was passed out on the sofa. "What the hell? I get invited, then ditched."

He popped the capsule he had been holding in his hand, grabbed a beer from the fridge, and turned the TV to a sports channel. He could have done this at home, instead he was a long walk away from his bed, and babysitting an unconscious chick.

Chapter 3

Condo complex

Ninety minutes later, Lucas was starving. A combination of drugs and athletic sex had sharpened his appetite. He pulled on his briefs and wandered into the kitchen in search of a snack, leaving Olivia snoring noisily on his king-sized bed. Thank God he didn't have to listen to that racket all the time. For a small person, she was obnoxiously loud.

In the living room, Noah was passed out and drooling in the large armchair, and Sarah was flopped facedown on the sofa, sound asleep. It was time to send everyone home so he could get a proper sleep.

"Wake up, sleepy head," Lucas sat beside Sarah and rested his hand on her back. He briefly considered exploring under her short shirt but didn't want her screaming rape. He lightly smacked her on the butt, "Sarah. Wake up. It's time to drive everyone home."

No response.

"Shit girl, you're really zonked-out," he said, shaking her shoulder. "Sarah, come on. Wake up!"

Noah sat up with a start, wiping drool from his chin. "Wha's going on?"

"What's all the shouting about?" Connor asked as he padded into the living room wearing a pair of Sacks boxers. He stretched and yawned, then scratched his crotch.

"I can't wake her up," Lucas said.

Connor reached for her shoulder and gave it a shake, "Sarah. Wake up." Puzzled, he put his fingers on her wrist. "I can't feel a pulse."

"What? No, you're just not doing it right," Lucas knocked Connor's hand away and put two fingers on her wrist, then frantically searched for the carotid artery in her neck. "It's faint, but there is a pulse. We have to get her out of here. Now!"

"We can't move her, she needs an ambulance," Connor said.

"Nope. When they see her, they'll call the cops and we can't have the cops here. Wake up the others, and we'll get her into the car. They can take her to the emergency ward."

Connor scowled at Lucas, then went to tell Hayley to get dressed. Lucas stormed into his bedroom, "Olivia, get out of bed. Now!" He pulled on pants and a shirt and stuffed his sockless feet into his shoes.

"What's the rush?" She turned her head on the pillow, one eye peering sleepily at Lucas.

"Get dressed. We have a problem."

She sat up, leisurely stretching her arms overhead, and deliberately exposing her breasts. "Come back to bed," she said, pulling the covers away from her body.

Lucas grabbed her upper arm and hauled her out of bed. "Get dressed. Your friend is sick. You are going to get her out of here."

"Jesus! Don't be so rough," Olivia squealed as her feet hit the floor.

"Get dressed!"

"Give me a minute, asshole."

He angrily swung his fist intending to punch her in the face, then stopped. A black eye or an imprint on her jawline would have the hospital staff asking awkward questions. He needed to keep this as uncomplicated as possible. His clenched fist stopped inches from her face. "Stop arguing," he threatened in a low voice.

Olivia bent her head and dressed as quickly as her trembling hands could manage.

"Lucas, this isn't going to work," Connor said as the men struggled to prop the unconscious woman between them. "There are cameras in the lobby and all the exits. They will record us literally dragging her through the lobby."

"I'll take my chances. Let's get her out of here."

Connor stopped. "No. Call an ambulance. She's in rough shape."

"Please, Lucas," Olivia begged. "Let me call an ambulance. You and Connor can leave. I'll say I had a key and knew I could find drugs here. Right, Hayley? You'll back me up on that?"

White-faced, Hayley nodded anxiously. "Yes. You had a key. Lucas didn't know we were coming over."

"And Noah? You agree too, right?" Olivia said.

"Yep. Sure. Whatever you say," he stammered, his eyes round with fear.

"That doesn't help with the cameras recording Connor and me leaving," Lucas countered.

"No one will think to look if I take the blame," Olivia said. She wasn't trying to be noble. She was flat-out terrified of Lucas. She'd experienced his temper before, but she had never seen this cold, uncaring anger.

"Fine, call the ambulance," he said, then flicked his head toward the sofa. "Let's put her back on the sofa." Lucas waited until Olivia had confirmed that an ambulance would be at the complex in under ten minutes then he grabbed her by both arms, his strong hands encircling her thin biceps. He gave her a sharp shake. "Remember what I told you before. Do. Not. Mess. With. Me. Keep your stories straight, and simple. This is your fault. You brought her here. And you thought it would be funny to see her messed up on drugs. Got it?"

Trembling, Olivia nodded. "Yes. I understand."

Roughly releasing her, he quickly searched in a kitchen drawer for his spare key, then jammed it in her palm. "Make sure you remember to show this to anyone who is asking nosey questions."

"I will. I promise." Trembling, she clamped her knees together, squeezing. *Don't pee. Don't pee. Don't pee.*

"Don't come back here. If you see me, don't speak to me. Got it?" He repeated.

"Yes."

He turned to Hayley and Noah and snarled. "Understand?"

They frantically nodded their heads.

Watching Lucas manhandle Olivia, Connor made up his mind. He'd leave the building until the ambulance crew took Sarah away, and then he was going to pack his shit and get as far away from Lucas as possible. Olivia's story of bringing her friends to the condo could have been believable, but now she'd have two hand-sized bruises on her upper arms. Hard to explain how she got those if Lucas wasn't home. Fricking LB, or Lucas, or Louis, or whatever the hell his real name was.

Connor's eyes swept over the accumulation of stolen electronics, e-bikes, and high-end clothing that they had taken in trade for drugs. He hated to leave it all behind, but couldn't fit either the kayak or a bicycle into his small vehicle, and he didn't have much use for the piles of expensive clothing.

It was time to move on. To put some distance between Lucas and himself.

Chapter 4

Penticton Regional Hospital

Olivia clung to the overhead grab handle in the front seat of the ambulance as it hurtled around a corner, turning sharply right onto Carmi Avenue. Even with the ear protectors on, she could hear the piercing scream of the siren. She wiped her nose and scrubbed at the tears running down her face.

I shouldn't have pressured Sarah into coming with us. No, it's not my fault. She should have refused that drink. This is her fault.

Drawn by morbid curiosity, Olivia turned slightly and looked over her left shoulder, trying to see what was happening with Sarah. The attendant was doing what looked like CPR, pressing forcefully on Sarah's exposed chest, and then using a plastic apparatus to pump air into her mouth. Repulsed, Olivia turned her eyes back to the route of the speeding vehicle.

The driver barreled into the parking lot and halted at the emergency entrance where two nurses and an empty stretcher were waiting. As they hustled Sarah inside, a tall red-haired woman approached Olivia.

"Hi, my name is Corporal Smith," she said displaying her identification. She refrained from overwhelming the young woman with her complete title, General Investigative Section of the Penticton RCMP, also known as GIS.

"Are you Olivia, the person who called for help?"

Olivia mutely nodded, wiping her eyes.

"I'll need a few details from you, Olivia. Let's go inside, okay?"

"My mom. I want my mom," Olivia whimpered.

"Yes, of course. What's her phone number?"

"I'll call her," Olivia's shaking finger pushed the button for her mother's number.

"Come inside," Caitlin Smith said, encouraging Olivia to follow her. Her eyes studied the traumatized young woman, searching for anomalies and clues. As an RCMP investigator, she knew nothing was ever as simple as it seemed. There were layers upon layers in every story.

"Mom, I need help," Olivia sobbed into her phone. "I'm at the hospital. Sarah is really sick." She listened, then answered, "No, Mom it can't wait. You have to come. There is a police officer who wants to talk to me," she said, shooting a guilty look at Caitlin. "Okay. I will."

"Is your mom coming?"

"She told me not to say anything until she gets here." Her eyes refused to meet Caitlin's.

"That's understandable. Let's go inside where it's warm. The cafeteria is closed, but we can find a somewhat drinkable cup of coffee at the nurses' station," she said.

"I don't drink coffee."

"Okay. We'll just find a warm quiet place to wait for your mom to arrive."

"Is Sarah going to be okay?" Olivia asked.

"I don't know. I haven't spoken to the doctor yet," Caitlin answered. She wasn't lying. She hadn't spoken to the doctor, but the ambulance attendant had shaken his head when their eyes had met over the stretcher. The trauma staff would try to revive her, but the attendant was certain that Sarah was technically DOA, dead on arrival. It was a waste of another young person's life.

It had been a busy night for Caitlin. This was her third call-out for an overdose. She had just finished a preliminary interview, and this call came in before she had even left the hospital. The holiday season put extra stress on everyone in emergency services. Police, fire, ambulance, and hospital staff were stretched thin and tired. There wasn't much *Ho Ho Ho* in the holiday season as lonely and unhappy people frequently attempted suicide at this time of the year.

She led Olivia to a relatively quiet spot, away from the organized frenzy of multitasking healthcare workers. She pointed at two seats and sat down. "We can wait here for your mom to arrive. Do you live far away?"

Olivia sniffed and shook her head. "No, not far, but they were sleeping, and they have to get dressed."

"Is your dad coming with her?" Caitlin asked when Olivia said they, instead of her.

"My mother's second husband is coming with her." She spat out the words.

"So, your stepdad?"

"His name is Kent. He's not my stepdad."

"I understand," Caitlin said. There seemed to be unresolved tensions in Olivia's family. "While we wait, Olivia, could you tell me your last name, home address, and telephone numbers?"

"Shouldn't I wait for Mom?"

"It's public information. I'm just trying to save time in case I have to respond to another problem."

"Caponera, that's my last name."

"And your contact information?"

She recited her address and cell number.

"How about a phone number for your mom? And her full name please."

"She was Stephanie Caponera but her second husband is Kent Ferguson, so that makes her Stephanie Caponera Ferguson," Olivia said firmly including her father's last name.

Chapter 5

Penticton Regional Hospital

"Olivia!" A voice shouted. "I told you to wait for me."

The girl swung around, with a guilty look, "Mom. I just told her my name and address. That's all. I swear."

Caitlin stood. "Good morning, Mrs. Ferguson. I'm Corporal Smith, General Investigative Section of the Penticton RCMP," she said using her full title this time.

The well-dressed brunette glared at Caitlin. "I specifically told her to wait. You should know that you can't question my daughter without me being present. My husband Kent Ferguson is an attorney." She indicated a man hovering behind her.

"A pleasure to meet you both. Olivia gave me her contact details," Caitlin said, "For the record, what is Olivia's birthdate?"

"Well, she's twenty, but just recently," Stephanie Ferguson hedged.

"Mom, I turned twenty, six months ago. I started work at the brewery when I was nineteen," Olivia said, then recited her birthdate to Caitlin.

"It doesn't matter. I told you to wait until I got here. Now, what is this about?"

"Corporal Smith?" A white-coated woman asked as she approached the group.

"Yes, that's me."

"May we have a word in private please?"

"I'm sorry, Mr. and Mrs. Ferguson, I need to speak to the doctor before we proceed with this conversation," Caitlin said and followed the doctor to an area where they could speak without being overheard.

"I'm Doctor Atwal," the dark-haired woman said, keeping her hands by her sides. Gone were the days when medical staff politely shook hands when they introduced themselves. "I'm afraid we couldn't save Sarah Wollman, the young woman who was admitted for a possible allergic reaction." She shook her head, slightly, and sighed. "This is her cellphone and her identification," she handed them to Caitlin. "Sarah was barely nineteen."

"Do you think it was an allergic reaction?" Caitlin pulled an evidence bag from her pocket and sealed the items inside, then pushed them deeper into a pocket, out of sight of the Fergusons. If they knew Caitlin had Sarah's phone, they might realize that something had happened to Sarah and be less willing to talk.

"We won't know for certain until the pathologist does an autopsy."

"Can you give me a hint?"

"I don't like guessing," Doctor Atwal said.

"But?"

"I think it was a combination of alcohol and drugs."

"Thank you. May I see Sarah before she is moved to the morgue?"

"I'm sorry, corporal, we're overloaded tonight. We've already transported her downstairs."

"I understand. I'll finish interviewing her friend first. Thank you, Doctor Atwal."

The woman nodded, and turned away, heading toward her next patient.

Caitlin returned to the family who were huddled around Olivia. "Olivia, do you know Sarah's home address?"

Olivia glanced at her mother, looking for permission to answer the question, and entirely ignoring Kent Ferguson who loomed silently behind his wife.

"Why?" Stephanie Ferguson demanded.

"Because I need to speak to her family," Caitlin said.

"She's fine, right?" Stephanie asked.

Hearing Stephanie's cold tone, Caitlin replied, "Mrs. Ferguson, would you want me discussing your daughter's medical information with a stranger?"

"Fine. Olivia, tell her."

"All I know is she lives in the Wiltse neighborhood," Olivia said. "I don't know her actual address."

"Thank you," Caitlin said. Closing her notebook, she looked at Kent Ferguson. "Mr. Ferguson, I am going to move this interview to the police station. Do you want Olivia to go home first and freshen up, or would you prefer we finish this now?"

"Why are you asking him? He's not my dad!" Olivia stated.

"Because I'm a lawyer," he answered, maintaining eye contact with Caitlin. "Isn't that right, Corporal Smith?"

"Yes, sir. Olivia may want to have legal representation for the next interview."

Kent studied Olivia. "Have you been up all night?"

She blushed and looked away. "I think I fell asleep for a few minutes." She couldn't admit to having sex with Lucas and passing out. She stuck her hand in her pocket, touching the hard metal of his spare key, and shivered.

"Are you okay, Olivia?" Kent Ferguson eyed his stepdaughter. "You look pale."

"Just a little tired," she said. She had to remember to show the spare key to the cop and tell the story that the four of them had entered the condo and raided Lucas's stash without his permission.

Stephanie gripped Kent's arm. "She needs to shower and sleep, then have a meal and fresh clothes."

He patted her hand but looked at Olivia. "Do you think you would sleep if we took you home right now?"

She shook her head. "No, I'm too worried about Sarah." While she did feel a bit badly that Sarah was sick, she was more concerned about Lucas's threats.

"Then we'll proceed with an interview at the police station, but if at any time I think Olivia needs to go home for a rest, I will stop the interview. Are we clear Corporal Smith?"

Caitlin nodded. "Yes, I understand. I'll meet you at the station in ten minutes."

Walking toward her vehicle, she contacted her co-worker Constable Ethan Jones. "Hey, are you available to sit in on an interview in ten?"

"Sure. I'm at my desk catching up on paperwork. Who are we interviewing?"

"Olivia Caponera, and her parents Stephanie Caponera Ferguson and Kent Ferguson."

"Ferguson. He's a criminal lawyer."

"Apparently."

"What's going on?"

"A possible drug overdose and the death of a young woman named Sarah Wollman," Caitlin said.

"Are we doing the NOK?" Ethan asked, referring to the next of kin notification that had to be done as soon as possible after a death.

"I want us to do this interview. Is there someone else available who can visit the parents?"

Ethan stood up and scanned the room. "Yep, Natalie is here," he said, then moved the phone away from his face, "Natalie, you got a minute?"

"What's up?" She asked walking toward Ethan.

"Are you okay to do a notification this morning?"

Natalie heaved out a breath. "A death notification on Christmas morning? Sure, I can do it. Was it a drug overdose?"

"Could be. Caitlin has a friend of the deceased, and her parents, coming in for a formal interview. She wants me to sit in on that, but the family of the deceased girl needs to be notified quickly. We don't want the news to get out on social media before they know about their daughter's death."

"Okay, give me the details and I'll find someone to come with me."

"I saw Evan Swan a few minutes ago. What about him?"

"Good idea. I'll go find Evan," she waved her phone at him. "Send me the information."

"Will do," he said, then turned back to his conversation with Caitlin. "Did you hear all of that? Natalie will take Evan, and they'll do the notification. Can you send her the contact info?"

"I only have a last name, Wollman. They live in the Wiltse area." Caitlin said.

"Okay, I'll tell Natalie to do a quick search before she heads out."

"I'll be back at the station shortly. I am just leaving the hospital."

"Where did the overdose happen?"

"At a party in a condo unit."

"Should we apply for a search warrant?"

"Yes, we'll have to get on that as soon as we interview Olivia."

"It's Christmas Day. Whichever judge we speak to isn't going to be happy."

"Can't be helped."

Chapter 6

The Naramata cottage

"I wish you could have come for Christmas," Jessica Sanderson said. Snuggled by a cozy fire, she smiled fondly at the image of her parents on her phone screen.

Gord Sanderson laughed. "And yet, you buggered off to Mexico as soon as we mentioned that we were coming for Christmas."

"I did not! I had my flight booked before you said that you *might* come for Christmas." Gently pushing aside torn wrapping paper and a pile of gifts from Mike, Jessica lifted her right leg and propped her aching foot on the coffee table.

"Don't listen to him, honey," Anne Sanderson said.

On her phone screen, she saw her mother edge her dad aside. "Your brothers thought it would be hilarious to surprise you and Mike. They wanted to arrive unannounced with all the fixings for a family-style turkey dinner," Anne said. "I'm glad we checked with you first before just showing up, otherwise Mike would have been stuck entertaining your rowdy relatives and our massive appetites."

"It would have been wonderful. I'm sorry I had already made plans to visit Yasmin and Carlos,"

Jessica's eyes roamed over their compact two-bedroom bungalow.

The cottage was equipped with a galley kitchen, a comfortable living-eating area, and a wood-burning fireplace that on cold winter days like today was a welcome addition. Having two full bathrooms helped, but adding her mom, dad, two large brothers, and their partners would push her hosting capabilities to the max. *Still, it would have been wonderful.*

"How about for New Year's Eve?" She cast a quick look at Mike, to see if he agreed. He nodded and gave her a thumbs-up.

"Can't. We are both working. But we could try for later in the year. Maybe February? Or March?"

"Either month would be great. If we plan ahead, Mike's assistants can take over in the winery for a few days. Then we could eat and drink our way around the valley."

"Are the winery restaurants open then?"

"Not really. Late April is when things get going," she said, hoping this winter wouldn't prove to be as destructive as last year's. The previous winter had been unseasonably warm late into December, providing little or no snow cover to protect the vines when the temperatures dropped to record-breaking lows in mid-January. Vineyards and orchards throughout the valley had been hit hard. Some vineyards had lost vast swaths of vines, necessitating a pull-out and re-planting. The cherry, peach, and apricot trees were barren. Vintners and orchardists were scrambling to keep their businesses afloat. A few of the wineries had closed their doors. Some temporarily, and others permanently, listing the properties for sale.

"Then let's aim for late April or early May," Anne said.

"That sounds good, Mom," she said, hoping the vineyards would survive and the fruit trees would be healthy and smothered in pink, white, and cream blossoms.

"So, tell us about your trip to Isla," Anne said.

Jessica flexed her scarred hand and wiggled the broken, but healing middle toe on her right foot. She angled the phone screen a smidge so that her parents couldn't see her signaling Mike to please keep quiet.

He grinned and jiggled his eyebrows. His version of a quiet threat to tattle.

"It was great. The weather was perfect. Warm, sunny, and no damn snow!" she said. "I finally got to meet my goddaughter, Yani. She's a charmer. Yasmin and Carlos send their love. As do Diego and Cristina. Everyone hopes that you will return to Isla soon."

Gord bellowed a laugh. "That's it? That's all you are going to tell us?"

"What do you mean, Dad?"

"Ten days in Mexico and your skin is still pasty-white. You were up to something, but I can wait for the real story. A bottle of wine or a couple of shots of tequila and you'll be babbling like a school kid."

"I don't babble," Jessica objected.

"Babbling like a school kid," he repeated. "Give Mike, and Sparky, a hug from both of us. Miss you pumpkin."

"Miss you too Dad. Love you, Mom."

"Love you too sweetie. And you, Mike."

"Right back at you," he said to Anne and Gord Sanderson, on the phone screen.

Chapter 7

The Naramata cottage

Jessica leaned back on the sofa. "Thank you for not ratting me out to my folks."

"Pretty hard to do when you still haven't told me what happened while you were in Mexico," Mike countered.

"I was too tired last night to get into details."

On the long drive from the Kelowna airport to their cottage in Naramata, she'd dozed off and Mike had let her sleep. When they arrived home, she'd stumbled in the door and headed straight to bed. Mumbling a sleepy goodnight to Mike, she'd asked him to make sure that Sparky had a final pee before he locked the door and turned out the lights.

"How about you tell me now?" he asked. He was smiling softly, as he normally did, but she could see in his eyes he was determined to know what had happened while she was on Isla Mujeres.

"Sure, but may I have the mimosa you promised me?" she asked, playfully batting her eyelashes at him.

"Coming right up, *princesa*."

She patted the sofa, signaling to Sparky that she wanted him to snuggle with her. He attempted to jump on the sofa, then sat down and looked at her. "Lazy faker. I know you can still make that jump. Come here Fuzz-butt," she said, standing to lift her solid, short-legged dog.

Setting Sparky on the sofa, she ran her hands over his wiry coat automatically checking for new bumps. He was somewhere around twelve or maybe thirteen years old, and he had developed several warts and lumps. Because of his congenital heart condition, his veterinarian was reluctant to anesthetize him for non-essential surgery, so the bumps were now part of his body structure. When asked, she usually described his fur color as white and brown tweed rather than merle, or dappled. The dark patches on his left side and rump matched the color of his long silky ears. His eyes were expressive. His nose was extraordinary. And it frequently got them into difficult situations.

"I missed you, pooch," she said giving him an unappreciated kiss on his snoot.

"How about me? Do I get a kiss too?" Mike asked, setting her drink on the table beside her.

"Anytime handsome. Pucker up."

He leaned over and kissed her, then moved to sit on the other side of Sparky. "Okay, enough delaying. Tell me how you acquired the scars on your hands and knees."

"I was walking from the restaurant to Yasmin's when a motorcycle rider hit my elbow and spun me toward the curb. I tripped and used my hands to stop me from doing a face-plant," she said. "My knees were scuffed up when I hit the ground.

"Ouch, painful," Mike sympathized, then rolled his hand. "Go on."

"What do you mean?"

"You've been trying to hide your limp. What else did you injure?"

"The middle toe on my right foot is broken."

"Middle toe? Usually, it's the big toe or the baby toe that takes the abuse when someone trips."

"I was wearing sandals, and my toe bent upwards when my foot struck the curb."

"That must have hurt like hell," he said.

"Yes, but I was close to Yasmin's house so I hobbled inside and cleaned myself up."

"Where were Yasmin and Carlos when this happened?"

"Still working at their restaurant, *A Pirate's Delight*. They arrived home later."

"Did the rider stop and offer to help you?"

"No." She shook her head, then sipped her mimosa to avoid his questioning gaze.

"Did you report him?"

"Well, no. not exactly. It turns out he is presumed to be dead."

"How?" He asked struggling to keep his voice calm.

"An unexplained airplane explosion when he was being transferred from a jail in Cancun to a jail in Florida. The pilots and two Florida deputies also died."

"Jesus, that's terrible. But jail and extradition? For leaving the scene of an accident?" Mike said. "That seems a bit excessive."

"He was going to be charged with murdering a young Florida woman."

Mike sighed and blew out his cheeks. "So, your chatty phone calls about the fun that you and Yasmin were having were BS? Instead, you were involved in a dangerous situation, again."

"I didn't want to worry you with details," she said reaching over Sparky to take Mike's hand. "A young woman was murdered. Diego and I got caught up in helping Sergeant Ramirez solve the murder."

"You and Diego, not Yasmin?"

"She's become a responsible mom."

"At least she is sensible," Mike gave her a frustrated look. "I know you frequently get involved in police investigations, but, dammit Jess, it scares the hell out of me when you do."

"I know."

He eyed her. "You're not going to change, are you?"

"Mike, you know I don't go looking for trouble."

"And yet it finds you."

She sat back. "Yes, it does."

He stood up. "I think I'll take a shower before I make us breakfast."

43

"Okay. I'll do the same," she said. "I haven't unpacked my suitcase yet, so I'll take my travel bag and use the guest bathroom."

"Fine," he said. Jessica could tell by the stiffness in Mike's expression that he was annoyed and trying very hard to maintain his Christmas spirit.

Despite being a long way from his family, she knew this was his favorite time of the year. He enjoyed inviting single friends and solo neighbors over for a carbohydrate-laden dinner and free-flowing beverages, and he spent months hunting for gifts for his parents, and now for Sparky and her.

Her attraction to danger was making him cranky, but her habit of meddling in police investigations might not be the only reason that he was irritated. A few days before her trip to Mexico, he had asked her to marry him.

She had replied, soon.

Not yes.

Not no.

Just soon.

Not because she didn't love him. She loved him so deeply she was afraid of ruining their romantic love story with marriage.

Explaining her reason to Mike had been interesting. He was a deep-rooted romantic and wanted to marry her. Mike and his first wife Lisa had been high school sweethearts, marrying soon after graduation. As they matured their interests diverged, and the marriage slowly died, ending in an amicable divorce.

In contrast, Jessica had a near-miss with, what was in her opinion an outdated tradition: marriage. Her financé, Alex, wanted a white picket fence, two dogs, and Jessica to be a stay-at-home mom caring for their kids. She loved to work and she loved to travel, and the baby showers held for her procreating gal-pals were an event to be endured, not enjoyed. When handed a squirming newborn, she smiled nervously and quickly passed the baby along to the next person. She realized she didn't have much in common with Alex except enjoyable sex. Their engagement ended before they had set the date.

And yet after explaining this to Mike, he still wanted to marry her!

She scooped her travel bag of toiletries out of her still-packed suitcase and headed to the guest bathroom. Sparky hopped off the couch and dragged his donut-shaped bed to block the bathroom doorway, preventing her from shutting the door.

"We've had this discussion before, pooch. When I shut the bathroom door, I don't magically disappear into a time portal. I'll still be in this room when I reopen the door," she said, holding one hand on the door and staring down at him. He wouldn't budge. "Okay, have it your way. Put your paws over your eyes if you don't want to see my girlie bits," she said, stripping off her clothes.

Jessica grinned when she heard Mike's voice from the other bathroom. "He's seen your girlie bits before and he approves."

His chin resting on the edge of his fluffy bed, Sparky intently watched as she stepped into the shower.

Chapter 8

Penticton RCMP station

Caitlin ushered Olivia and the Fergusons into an interview room. Sitting down she re-introduced herself on the recording equipment, then waited for Ethan to do the same.

"Constable Ethan Jones, General Investigative Section of the Penticton RCMP," he said.

Once the others had stated their names, she read the legal caution and began the interview.

"Olivia, tell me in your own words about last night."

Kent Ferguson interrupted immediately, "I prefer that you ask her straightforward questions," he said. The last thing he needed was his tired, scared stepdaughter rambling on and on, possibly incriminating herself.

"Alright," Caitlin said. "Then who owns the condo where you were last night?"

"I don't know. Lucas just rents it," she said, letting her chin drop toward her chest.

"And what is Lucas's last name?" Caitlin asked.

"I don't know. I never asked," Olivia mumbled.

"You'll have to speak more clearly for the recording, Olivia. I'll repeat the question. What is Lucas's last name?"

"I don't know," she said loudly.

"Was Lucas home?"

"No, he's out of town for Christmas," she quickly pulled out the spare key. "I had a key to his condo. He gave it to me."

Caitlin caught the brief look of surprise in Kent Ferguson's eyes. The key was news to him. She reached for an evidence bag and opened it, "please drop the key in the bag."

Olivia shot a worried glance at Kent, and he nodded. "Do it."

"Are you close friends with Lucas?" Caitlin asked setting the key and bag on the table.

"No, not really."

"Then why did he give you a key?"

"He said I could come by and just chill. Listen to music. Watch TV."

"Don't you have access to a TV at home?"

"Yes, but it's boring hanging around there all the time by myself." She pinged a sulky look at her mother. "She's always busy with her fundraising job. Or going to fancy events with him." She angrily pointed her chin at Kent Ferguson.

Caitlin glanced at the Fergusons. Stephanie was flushed with embarrassment, while Kent maintained a detached expression. The heated family discussion would happen later, in the privacy of their home.

"How old is Lucas?"

"I don't know, I never asked."

"But older than you?"

"Yes. I guess."

"A lot older?"

"I said I never asked."

Caitlin studied Olivia for a moment. Those units didn't rent cheaply, and the landlord would be wary of renting to anyone under the age of twenty-five, but Olivia wasn't forthcoming, so she switched tactics. "Did you and Sarah arrive together?"

"Yes. Sarah offered to drive us," she said. *Offered sounded nicer. More willing.* As if Sarah was excited to be going with them, instead of reluctant and whiny about how she wanted to spend Christmas Eve with her parents and her annoying younger brother. *This will be the last time I include her.*

"Us? Was someone else there?"

"Hayley. And Noah. We all work part-time at the Cactus."

"Do you mean Cactus Brewing," Caitlin asked.

"Yeah. Me and Hayley are servers in the taproom, and Noah works in the brewery."

"What about Sarah? What is her job?"

"She works in the kitchen as the dish pig," Olivia said.

"Why do you call her the dish pig?" Caitlin asked.

"It's the industry nickname for a person who scrapes the dishes, and loads the dishwasher," Olivia replied.

"I see. Where are Hayley and Noah now?"

"When I called 911, Hayley went home by taxi. I'm not sure where Noah went. Maybe he rode with Hayley. But I stayed with Sarah, all the way to the hospital," she said, straightening up and smiling proudly at Caitlin.

She's expecting praise. "I'll need their full names and contact information, too," Caitlin noted Olivia's deflated expression when she didn't applaud her for accompanying her comatose friend to the hospital. She slid a notepad and pen across the table and waited while the young woman printed names, phone numbers, and street names.

"I'm not sure of their exact addresses," Olivia said, pushing the notepad back.

"Does Lucas keep a lot of drugs in his condo?" Caitlin asked.

"I...um...I'm not sure."

"We are in the process of obtaining a search warrant for Lucas's apartment," Caitlin said, mentally adding. *As soon as I am done here.* "Are we going to find more than a personal supply of drugs?"

"Stop right there. Why are you applying for a search warrant?" Kent Ferguson demanded.

Surprised that he hadn't twigged sooner, Caitlin answered. "I regret to inform you that Sarah Wollman passed away this morning. We are in the process of contacting her parents. I ask that you have compassion for the Wollman family, and do not tell anyone, nor post anything on social media."

Shocked, Olivia burst into tears, "Mom! I want to go home. I don't want to answer any more questions."

Kent Ferguson closed the binder where he'd been making notes. "We're done here, Corporal Smith. You should have told us about Sarah Wollman before we entered the interview room. Olivia needs to rest before we resume."

"Interview suspended at o-nine-thirty-hours. Corporal Caitlin Smith," she said.

Ethan added, "Constable Ethan Jones."

When the recording was off, Stephanie Ferguson surged to her feet and leaned over the table pointing her finger at Caitlin's face. "That was despicable, Ms. Smith. You could have broken the news to Olivia more gently."

"My title is Corporal Smith, Mrs. Ferguson, and your daughter Olivia is an adult," she said with a touch of steel in her voice. "Sarah Wollman, who was younger than your daughter, died tonight and we need to find out how and why."

Caitlin turned her unwavering gaze on Kent Ferguson and handed him her RCMP contact card.

"Please phone me as soon as Olivia has rested so that we can continue this interview."

"Don't be ridiculous, it's Christmas Day!" Stephanie Ferguson shouted, pulling her sobbing daughter closer.

"Yes, it is. And we have to inform Sarah Wollman's parents that their daughter will not be coming home Christmas Day, or any other day." Caitlin replied evenly. She wanted to yell at the entitled, insensitive woman, but that would only exacerbate the situation.

"That's not Olivia's fault," Stephanie shouted, her blotchy face jutted angrily toward Caitlin.

"Stephanie, this isn't helping," Kent Ferguson said. "We'll discuss this at home."

"Please contact me as soon as possible to resume this interview," Caitlin said.

Ethan Jones followed the family, escorting them out the side door. When he returned, Caitlin was sitting at her desk clutching an empty coffee mug. The cup clicked repeatedly on her desktop as her hands trembled.

"Are you okay?" He asked.

She lifted her chin, "I'm bloody furious at that woman's callous attitude. She doesn't give a hot damn about Sarah, or her heartbroken family. We don't even know if Sarah has siblings or grandparents. We just know she's young, and she's dead, and Olivia Caponera took her to a place where they had no business being."

Ethan picked up the evidence bag with the single key and stared at it. "What building were they in?"

"The set of towers, down by the lake. Why?"

"I could be wrong, but I think you also need a key fob to access any of the entrances, and the elevators," he said.

"You mean like a car fob?" Caitlin mimed pointing an electronic key and thumbing a button.

"No, those small grey discs that you touch to an electronic reader. They're common in high-rises."

"Right, sorry, I'm tired," she said. "Then how did they get inside without a key fob?"

He shrugged. "Someone could have let them in, but then that same person would also have to push the elevator button for the correct floor. The electronic system is designed to keep unwanted strangers from accessing the residential floors."

"You would think four young people arriving late on Christmas Eve, without an access fob, would be a concern to other residents."

"I guess Olivia could have said they were visiting her grandparents or some such thing."

Caitlin snorted. "Any grandparent that I know is in bed well before ten o'clock."

He chuckled. "True. Did Olivia say what time they entered the condo?" He asked.

"It was one-thirty when the ambulance arrived at the hospital with Sarah," she said. "I didn't have a chance to ask what time they arrived at the condo before her mother appeared and demanded that I stop questioning Olivia."

"What I don't understand is why they weren't home on Christmas Eve with their families," Ethan said.

"You heard Olivia. She made it quite clear that she did not want to be with her mother and stepdad. But, the other three? I have no idea, yet," she checked her phone for missed messages. "Any word from Natalie about the NOK?"

"Not yet," he shook his head. "She was planning to head home for a few hours sleep, as soon as they had finished the notification."

"Right, and we should do the same. I can find someone else to sit in on Olivia's interview once Kent Ferguson gives me the go-ahead. You should spend Christmas Day with Meaghan and Rowan," she said. "I bet he's excited about opening his presents."

"He's still too young. There will be a lot of excited giggling and laughter when we help him rip the paper off of his gifts, but he's not old enough to be hyperactively jumping on our bed or running through the house," Ethan said. "I'm just grateful that his health concerns have disappeared, and he's a strong and healthy little boy."

"Me too. Now get going. I'll see you tomorrow."

"Call if you need me." He leaned in and pecked her cheek. "Merry Christmas."

"You too. Give my love to Meaghan and Rowan." She looked at her phone again. Still nothing from Natalie. She'd wait for fifteen more minutes then text, to see how she and Evan were doing with the NOK.

In the meantime, she would run a background check on the condo address to see if she could find the elusive Lucas, whoever he is.

Chapter 9

The Naramata cottage

Jessica set Sparky's plate on his washable mat, theoretically designed to keep his mess off the floor. From the first day that the scrawny, tick-infested stray had entered her life, he had refused to eat from a bowl. She assumed that he was accustomed to eating off the ground, or from a garbage can, and didn't like the sensation of his whiskers touching the sides of the bowl. Unable to communicate in her language, he hadn't been able to confirm, or deny, her theory.

Unlike any other dog that Jessica had known, Sparky rarely cleaned his plate or the surrounding area where bits and pieces had been licked over the edge. He ate what he wanted and left the mess for his staff to clean up, she, of course, being the staff.

With a nod to his Mexican roots, his everyday blue melamine plate had been replaced with a festive red ceramic plate emblazoned with *Feliz Navidog!* "Feliz Navidad, pooch," she said. "Scrambled eggs for breakfast, and later, there will be a small piece of turkey for you."

Frying pan in hand, Mike looked down at Sparky. "What are you waiting for? I soft scrambled those eggs just for you."

"He's waiting to see if we are having something better." Leaning against the counter she typed a brief text to her friend, Caitlin Smith. *Merry Christmas, chica. Are you still coming for dinner?* Putting her phone on the counter she set the table for breakfast. Her phone pinged with an incoming text.

Hope so. Super busy. Working on a case. C

Come when you can. Mike says Merry Xmas.

Merry Xmas to you and Mike. And Fuzz-butt.

"Caitlin is busy with a case, but she is still hoping to come for dinner tonight," Jessica said to Mike. "She says Merry Christmas to you and the Fuzz-butt."

"I'm glad she is coming. We haven't seen her for a bit," he said, lifting two over-easy eggs onto a warmed plate. He added a couple of strips of extra-crispy bacon and a scoop of hash browns. "Breakfast is served, señorita," he said handing her the plate.

"Gracias, mi amor," she set the plate down, then broke one strip of bacon in half and crumbled it over Sparky's scrambled eggs.

Mike joined her and raised his refreshed mimosa. "Happy Christmas my love. Here's to many more."

"Yes, many more." She sipped, then put the glass down. "I'm starving."

"I can't imagine being a cop at Christmas," Mike said, loading his fork with egg and bacon.

"It's a tough time of year for all first responders and medical staff," Jessica said.

"Did she say what's going on?"

"No, just a quick text that she's still working but will try to come for dinner."

"I thought she was on the night shift and off for Christmas Day," he said.

"She was, but something important must have come up," Jessica checked her phone for the time. "She's worked at least three hours longer than normal." She glanced at Sparky who was still sitting beside his plate, but looking at her. "That's all there is pooch, bacon, and eggs. Or if you prefer, I can replace it with your regular dog food," she threatened.

"Fuff," Sparky snorted and stood to eat. He slowly and carefully picked the bacon off the eggs, ate the bacon first, and then licked up most of the scrambled eggs. A few bits dropped over the side and onto the mat.

Mike's laughing eyes met hers.

"He is unique," she said.

"He's weird," he replied.

"One of a kind," she said. "What time do we have to put the turkey in for dinner tonight?"

"We?"

"Okay, what time are you planning to put the turkey in?"

"That depends on when we are expecting Caitlin to arrive?"

"Huh, I don't think we discussed that. I'm assuming around five, cocktail time."

"If we aim for serving dinner at six, the turkey should go in the oven around three."

"What do you want me to do?"

"Set the table, chill the wine, and prep the veggies."

"It's a deal."

Chapter 10

Wollman's home

Constables Natalie Garcha and Evan Swan parked their squad cars in front of a modest home in the original development of the Wiltsie neighborhood. Along the street, a multitude of Christmas lights twinkled in the shrubbery. Inflatable plastic Santas, reindeer, trains, and snowmen waved and wobbled as small compressors noisily blew air into the blowup figures. The neighborhood looked to be about thirty years old, well-maintained, and comfortable.

Higher up the hillside, the newer homes were larger, grander covering most of the available space on the lot. Floor-to-ceiling windows, dark wood, and white stone were the preferred materials. She liked the cozier feel of the older neighborhood.

Natalie sent a text to Evan, sitting in the squad car beside hers. *Ready?*

Not really. He replied.

Me neither. She opened the driver's door, and stepped out. She straightened her cap, and tugged the hem of her jacket down. Delaying.

Evan stepped out of his vehicle and made similar adjustments to his coat, then nodded briskly at her.

In silence, they walked the recently shoveled driveway and tapped on the front door. A cheery Santa Claus wreath hung on the glossy red door.

It opened, suddenly. A red-eyed woman clutched the handle as her frantic eyes swept over the uniformed figures standing on her doorstep. "Where is she? Sarah didn't come home last night. Where is my baby girl?"

"Mrs. Wollman?" Natalie asked.

"Yes," she confirmed. "Has there been an accident? I've been calling my daughter's phone every few minutes, but she's not answering," she blurted. "I didn't want her to go out last night."

"I'm Constable Garcha, and this is Constable Swan. May we please come in?"

"Why?"

"Please Mrs. Wollman. May we come in?"

"Irene? Honey, what's wrong?" A heavy-set, man appeared behind her. His thick hair was receding, leaving a ring of reddish-blonde hair.

"Mr. Wollman?"

"Yes, I'm Ed Wollman, and this is my wife, Irene."

Natalie said, "May we please come inside, sir?"

"Let them in darling," he said gently wrapping an arm around his wife and pulling her away from the door.

"Sarah's fine, I know she is. She's fine," Irene shook her head, dislodging the pile of long greying hair that had been trapped on top of her head in a messy bun.

"Come on darling," his voice trembled.

Natalie and Evan stamped the salty snow from their footwear and stepped inside. "Would you like us to remove our boots?" she asked.

"No, it's fine," he said. "Please come into the kitchen." He led Irene to the kitchen table and pulled out a chair. "Sit down, love."

He stood beside his wife with a hand resting gently on her shoulder. "What's happened?"

Natalie's heart thumped against her ribs, as she willed her voice to remain steady. "I am so sorry Mr. and Mrs. Wollman. Sarah passed away early this morning at the hospital."

"No. No. No. Not my baby. It can't be my baby," Irene wailed. She jammed her face against her husband's stomach.

"Are you sure?" Ed asked, absently soothing his wife's hair with one hand.

"Yes sir, she had her driver's license as identification. And her friend Olivia Caponera confirmed her name."

"Was she in a car accident? She just recently got her driver's license," Ed Wollman said. "She's a very careful driver, but this is her first time driving in winter conditions. And the deer. They're a menace. All over the roads at night. I don't know why the city can't deal with the problem," he said, the words spilling out. "Did she hit a deer?"

"I don't know the exact cause, but she was brought in by ambulance from a condo."

"What? Whose condo?" Ed asked.

"I'm sorry sir, we weren't given that information. We know that Sarah was with her friend Olivia, and two other young people at a party. Something happened, and an ambulance was called for Sarah," Natalie said. "That's all that I know at the moment, sir. I am so very sorry for your loss," she said, knowing how trite that phrase sounded. Words could never soothe a shattered heart.

Ed Wollman slumped into a chair. "It can't be true. Sarah is only nineteen. She has plans to attend UBC next semester, to study Environmental Sciences. She wants to make a difference in our world."

Noting Ed's reluctance to speak of his daughter in the past tense, Evan said, "I am so sorry for your loss Mr. and Mrs. Wollman. Is there someone we can call, to be with you?"

Ed lifted his eyes and shook his head. "No. There's just the four of us. Sarah and Logan are our world."

"Oh my God, how are we going to tell Logan?" Irene moaned. "He adores his big sister."

"We'll tell him together, love," Ed replied, wiping his wide hand over his face. "That's what families do. Face the bad times together."

A teenage version of Ed Wollman suddenly appeared in the kitchen doorway. Presumably, this was their son, Logan. The teen's confused and frightened expression told Natalie that he had overheard at least part of the conversation.

"Dad? What's happened to Sarah?" He asked.

"Oh, Logan, what are we going to do?" his mother wailed. "Sarah's gone. She's gone."

Chapter 11

Caitlin and Natalie

How did the notification go? Caitlin's text to Natalie, was followed by, *Are you OK?*

Natalie thumbed a reply. *I'll call.* She tapped Caitlin's number, "Hi, it's done, and it was awful."

"I am so sorry you and Evan had to do that. It should have been me," Caitlin said.

"No, you had to interview Olivia while the information was still fresh in her mind. How did that go?"

"Not well," Caitlin said. "I got shut down pretty quickly. Olivia has gone home for a rest. We'll continue later this afternoon. In the meantime, I'm searching for information on the guy that lives in the condo unit. I've finally figured out his last name, Bankole. Lucas Bankole. And surprise, surprise, he has an outstanding warrant for not showing up at his trial."

"Trial for what?"

"Possession for the purpose of trafficking."

"Huh. Nice guy," Natalie said. "Hey, aren't you off today?"

"Death doesn't take holidays, Nat."

"I know, but you've been working ridiculously long hours lately."

"Doesn't matter. I'm not a big fan of the holiday season. My folks are back in Ontario and most of my friends are married and celebrating with their own families."

"Come to my house. We always have too much food," Natalie offered.

"That's kind of you. I have already accepted a dinner invitation with Jessica and Mike. I just sent her a text to update her that I'm working but hoping to get there on time."

"That's good."

"Are you on your own?" Caitlin asked, thinking that maybe she should ask Jessica if Natalie could join them for Christmas dinner.

Natalie chuckled. "Me? Never. I'm Sikh, so I'm never totally alone. My mom and dad, and extended family are always nearby. During our religious celebrations, there is always too much delicious food heaped on tables, too many relatives all talking at the same time, and too many elderly aunties trying to matchmake for me. In my family, it's incomprehensible for a woman in her twenties to be single and have a career."

Caitlin smiled at Natalie's description of her family. "My mother has tried several times to find me an economically suitable mate from an appropriate family. She doesn't care if I love the man or not, he just has to have a good career and be able to provide for me."

Natalie chuckled. "That sounds familiar. Are you certain that you weren't born into a Sikh family?"

"It might have been more fun," Caitlin replied. "I have been a cop for ten years, and my mother still refuses to tell anyone. If anyone asks, she says that I work for a large federal corporation. It's one of the reasons I am happy to live on the other side of the country. I'm far away from her arched eyebrows and her muttered, 'Oh Caitlin, what were you thinking?"

"If you are interested, I have several tall and very handsome cousins who are single," Natalie said. "I could introduce you."

"Matchmaker for another ambitious female cop? That would distress your aunties," Caitlin replied.

Natalie sighed lightly. "Yes, you're right. I love my family to pieces, but they can test my patience."

"Mine too," Caitlin replied, then quietly added, "I can't imagine the pain the Wollman family is feeling right now."

"Their son, Logan, overheard us talking in the kitchen. He was shattered. Sarah was his older sister and only sibling."

"Poor kid," Cailin said. "Head home, Nat. I'll see you on your next shift."

"Take care, and Merry Christmas to you Caitlin."

"Thanks, same to you. Or is that the wrong thing to say?"

"Merry Christmas is fine. Talk later."

Chapter 12

Fergusons, driving home

"What were you thinking?" Stephanie Ferguson slammed the door of their dark blue Range Rover and rounded on her daughter who had slunk into the back seat.

"I just wanted to be with my friends, and get away from you...and him," Olivia snapped.

"I see. So, how did that go? Did you suddenly decide to pop into a stranger's home on Christmas Eve and help yourself to his drug supply?"

"He's not a stranger. He's a friend."

"A friend," Stephanie said using air quotes. "A friend who is much older, and whom we've never met."

"You can't be bothered to find out anything about my other friends, so why would you care about meeting Louis?" Olivia shouted.

"You told the police his name is Lucas, and now you are calling him Louis. Which is it?" Stephanie demanded.

"I'm tired and confused, and I've heard him use both names," Olivia said.

"And that didn't concern you? That your so-called friend uses multiple names?"

"Maybe it's a nickname. I don't know. Leave me alone."

Kent turned to look at Olivia. "Watch your attitude, young lady. Don't speak to your mother like that."

Stephanie touched her husband's arm and lightly shook her head letting him know, that although she appreciated his concern, this was her battle, not his.

"I don't have to listen to you! You are not my dad," Olivia said, jamming her earbuds into her ears.

"Oh, no, we are not done yet," Stephanie reached behind and pulled the earbuds out. "Your friend died. You took her to that condo. The police will try to make you responsible for this mess," Stephanie said. "Yet despite your rotten attitude, Kent is willing to defend you against possible criminal charges. You should be grateful!"

Olivia simpered sarcastically. "Oh, thank you, Kent. Whatever would I do without you? You are so kind, thank you so much."

"Olivia! Apologize right now!" Stephanie clenched her hands together, fighting the urge to reach behind and slap her daughter's face. She was a spoiled pain in the ass, whom Stephanie adored, yet frequently disliked.

Ignoring her mother, Olivia said, "Sarah is not my friend. She had a car, so I asked her to drive us to the condo. I don't hang out with her. She's boring."

"Who is now dead because of your irresponsible actions," Stephanie stated.

"You are a horrible person!" Olivia snatched the earbuds from her mother and stuffed them back in her ears. Slumping down, she squeezed her eyes shut and turned her tear-streaked face toward the side window.

Stephanie blew out a sigh. "Let's go home."

Kent started the vehicle and steered out of the RCMP parking lot toward their house; a house that didn't feel very homey to him, lately. It was time for Olivia to move out on her own, even if he had to subsidize her rent. That was assuming she wasn't incarcerated for criminal negligence in the death of Sarah Wollman. Olivia was legal age, and that could make a big difference if this went to court. *What the hell had happened at that condo?*

Kent looked over at Stephanie. "Do you know anything about Noah or Hayley?"

She shrugged. "Not really. I have only been to Cactus once, and I saw Olivia talking to Hayley, but that's about it. I don't remember meeting Noah."

"How old is Hayley?"

"Not sure, but she would have to be at least nineteen to work in the taproom. Why?"

"Just trying to get a handle on the situation," he replied. "Any thoughts on her personality? Reliable? Flaky?"

"It's been a tough morning. Let's just get home and relax for a bit," she said tilting her head to motion that they should talk about this privately.

"Go ahead, *Mother*. Feel free to criticize my best friend. A friend that you have never spoken more than five words to," Olivia sniped from the backseat.

"Olivia, let it go. We're all stressed and tired," Stephanie replied, then lapsed into silence.

"And a very Merry fricking Christmas to all!" Olivia muttered.

Kent's hands tightened on the steering wheel, as he stared straight ahead.

Before the Range Rover had come to a complete stop inside their three-car garage, Olivia opened her door and scrambled out.

"Olivia, stop," Stephanie shouted to her daughter's retreating back as she slammed the door leading into the kitchen. "Dammit!"

Kent put the car in park and shut if off. He tapped the down button on the garage door remote and turned to face his wife. "She has to take responsibility for her actions."

"I know, she can be a pain in the butt. She's young. She'll grow out of it."

"She's not a kid anymore, Steph. She's an adult," he said. She could be held responsible for the death of Sarah Wollman."

"It's a very sad situation but it's not Olivia's fault. I'll send flowers to her family."

"Flowers? Stephanie do you not understand how serious this situation is?"

"Well, it looks bad for all of us, but we'll weather it. We are a strong family unit."

He tipped his chin and studied her face. "I'm not referring to our reputations. I meant the very real possibility that Olivia will be charged in connection to Sarah's death."

"Don't be dramatic, Kent. Sarah probably had a bad reaction to whatever drugs she took. I told you. It's not Olivia's fault."

"We don't know that. Olivia hasn't been forthcoming with details."

"Then maybe we should hire someone else to represent her. Someone she's more comfortable talking to."

He jerked back. "Don't you trust me to defend Olivia?"

"She's my daughter, and I must do what's best for her. She doesn't respond well to you."

"Whatever you want. I can make some phone calls," he said as he opened his door, and stepped out of the car. He pulled in a deep breath, held it for a few seconds, and exhaled. Hiding his anger, he carefully closed the driver's side door, and turned away from his wife, entering their house through the kitchen. He heard her come in about a minute later.

"Olivia?" Stephanie called down the hallway, shouting over the loud music coming from her daughter's bedroom. "I'm making breakfast. What would you like?"

The music increased in volume.

"Olivia! Turn that down, or use your earbuds," she shouted.

The noise stopped abruptly.

"And now, she's probably blasting it through her earbuds, and permanently damaging her hearing," Stephanie muttered to herself. "Kent? Are you hungry?" She opened the refrigerator door and stared listlessly at the shelves, laden with supplies for their Christmas dinner.

"Not right now. I'll make something later," he said, pouring himself a stiff drink.

"What about the turkey? Should I still cook it for dinner?"

"Whatever you think is best," he said.

She shut the refrigerator door, then reopened it and pulled out an open bottle of wine. "I need this," she said pouring herself a large glass.

Kent stretched out on the sofa, a glass of whiskey and ice on a side table and considered which lawyer to call. Someone good with criminal cases. And someone who wouldn't be annoyed about an interrupted Christmas.

Chapter 13

Penticton RCMP station

"Corporal Smith, this is Kent Ferguson," he said when Caitlin answered the phone.

"Hello, Mr. Ferguson. Are you ready to resume Olivia's interview?" She glanced at the clock on her computer. There was still time to do the interview, then scoot home for a shower and a change of clothes, before dinner at Jessica's. Sleep would have to wait until after dinner.

"Not unless you have sufficient cause to arrest her."

Dammit.

"I don't understand, Mr. Ferguson. When you were here this morning, you were willing to let her speak to me," Caitlin replied.

"That was before we knew that Sarah Wollman had accidentally died at the party," he said. "We have engaged Leonard McCarthy as legal council for Olivia. My wife and I feel that I am too personally involved to represent our daughter."

"That's your right to make a change in legal representation, sir, but I still don't understand why we can't get this cleared up today?"

"As my wife pointed out, it's Christmas Day. We feel Olivia needs time with her family to recover from the shock of her friend's death. I've arranged for Mr. McCarthy to be available on December 26th or 27th. Your choice."

"My choice is today, Mr. Ferguson."

"That's not going to happen unless you have sufficient cause to arrest her," he repeated, with calm certainty.

"Alright. Tomorrow morning at nine."

"Fine. See you then."

Disconnecting the call, Caitlin smacked her palm on her desk. "Fricking Leonard McCarthy," she muttered remembering her encounter with the brilliant, and arrogant, criminal attorney on a previous case.

As for this case, she'd tried obtaining a search warrant for the condo but hadn't found a judge who was available to sign the paperwork on Christmas Day. She'd have to try again tomorrow. They still hadn't been able to find Lucas Bankole, the renter. In the meantime, the unit had been sealed off and a uniform cop had been stationed outside the door to prevent anyone from entering.

Suddenly a wave of exhaustion swept over her. She turned off the computer and shrugged into her jacket. Picking up her keys she nodded at the civilians who staffed the front, taking complaints and reports. "I'm heading home. I desperately need some sleep. Merry Christmas to both of you," she said, waving goodbye as she walked away.

"Merry Christmas, Caitlin," they responded. "Have a drink for us."

"Will do."

Opening the door of her two-bedroom townhouse, her small black and white cat yowled loudly. Tickle's bright yellow eyes glared accusingly at Caitlin. Nicknamed Tickle the Terrible, she was a churlish humane society rescue that slashed anyone's hands if they touched her soft furry tummy, yet she craved human company.

"I'm sorry I left you so long, princess. Did you nearly starve to death?" she asked the cat. "If my workmates heard me talking to you, they'd realize that I am a crazy cat lady." She checked the self-feeding station, and Tickle's water dispenser. Both were fine, but the litter box was dotted with large lumps of buried poop.

Meowing dolefully, Tickle butted her head against Caitlin's calf.

"I know, I know. You're lonely."

That was a fairly accurate description of her life too. She was lonely, damn lonely.

Two years ago, she had been promoted and transferred from the larger city of Winnipeg to the smaller rural-based city of Penticton where the singles scene was practically non-existent, and everyone was naturally cautious around new police officers. Being an unattached cop had its challenges, but being an unattached female cop was doubly intimidating for many men.

Maybe a coffee date with one of Natalie's cousins wouldn't be a terrible idea.

Removing her boots and jacket, Caitlin quickly scooped the lumps out of Tickle's litter box and deposited them in a garbage can. "How about some salmon Fancy Feast for a Christmas treat? It's your favorite," Caitlin said. She opened a fresh can and dabbed a tablespoon into Tickle's dish then set it on the floor.

Tickle strutted over to the dish and sniffed. She silently studied Caitlin between slow blinks, then flicked her tail and strutted away.

"We've had this conversation before. Unless you can open a tin, that's all there is on tonight's menu," she said, putting the remainder of the can inside the fridge. "You'll have to make do with your kibble."

The cat sat down ten feet away and stared reproachfully at her.

"Alright. Come here for a quick cuddle, then I desperately need a shower and a nap." She picked up her cat and plopped onto the sofa, acutely conscious that her hands were in danger of being shredded at any moment should she touch the no-go zone.

Within minutes, Caitlin's eyelids were drifting closed, and she forced herself to move into her bedroom. Sleep first. Shower later.

Tapping a message to Jessica, she wrote. *Just got home. Need sleep. What's the latest I can arrive?*

5:30 or 6:00?

That works. See you soon.

She set the alarm on her phone and snuggled under her soft duvet. Her thoughts slowly drifted toward sleep as she felt Tickle jump on the bed. Purring loudly the cat began to knead her pillow. Making biscuits, as her nana used to say. The repetitive motion and rhythmic purring soothed her to sleep.

Seemingly seconds later, a loud persistent beeping that sounded exactly like a large truck backing up toward her bed, dragged her awake. She stabbed the phone, shutting off the offensive beeping, and swung her feet to the floor. "Shower. Fresh clothes. A bit of makeup, and go. But you are not invited," she said to Tickle.

Twenty minutes later, Caitlin took a quick look at her outfit in the full-length mirror. Wearing a deep red roll-neck sweater, over skinny black pants, and classy black ankle boots she looked pretty good. "You'll do," she said.

Her phone pinged as she reached for her dressy jacket.

Merry Christmas, Caitlin. Hope you have a great one. Harley.

"What the heck? I haven't talked to Harley Chan in months," she said, texting him a reply. *Thanks! Same to you. You still VPD?*

Yep. Investigating homicides. You?

Same. Late for Xmas dinner. Can I call tomorrow?

Absolutely. Enjoy.

Thanks. Merry Xmas to you.

Chan had originally contacted her the previous year when two of their cases had intersected. When he introduced himself, saying his first name was Harley she thought he meant he liked Harley motorcycles. Nope. His name was Harley Chan, which sounded like Charlie Chan, the heroic but fictional Honolulu police detective popular in the 1920s. Laughing lightly she explained how the humorous association had popped into her head.

He had dryly responded. "Wow. I've never heard that before."

Their infrequent calls and texts had slowly changed from strictly police business to witty messages. She pocketed her phone, thinking that she should make the effort to do something other than send him the occasional message. Like drive to Vancouver and meet him for dinner and drinks. It was something to think about.

Recognizing Caitlin's dressy black jacket as the signal that she was once again leaving, Tickle yowled in protest.

"I'll bring you a little piece of roast turkey as your Christmas treat," she said to the complaining cat.

If a cat could do a one-finger salute, Caitlin was certain Tickle was doing it. The cat resented being left on her own for long stretches, and this was turning into a very long stretch.

Chapter 14

The Naramata cottage

Slouching comfortably on the sofa, Jessica reached for Mike's hand and gave it an affectionate squeeze. "You outdid yourself, sweetie. Dinner was amazing."

He lifted their linked hands and carefully avoiding her healing fingers, he kissed her palm. "Any meal that you don't have to cook is, in your words, amazing," he teased.

"Maybe," Jessica agreed, resting her aching foot on the coffee table.

When Caitlin arrived, she'd noticed Jessica's limp and had asked what had happened. Jessica's vague reply had been enough to satisfy her sleep-deprived curiosity.

"Yes, thank you, Mike," Caitlin said, gently twirling her glass of wine. "It was delicious. It's been a few years since I've had a turkey feast like that."

With the heat of the crackling fire saturating her bones, the resiny aroma of a real Christmas tree titillating her memory bank, and the schmaltzy songs playing through the music app on the television, the tension in Caitlin's shoulders melted away. She was pleasantly full, and about to slide into a drowsy food coma.

"When did you last spend Christmas with your folks?" He asked.

"A while ago," she murmured.

"How long?"

"Several years."

"Why?"

"Let it go. I'm enjoying this," Caitlin responded, sleepily.

"Okay. Another time."

"Can you tell us anything about the case that you are working on?" Jessica asked. She'd struggled to not interrogate Caitlin while they devoured the scrumptious food, but now that dinner was over, she was fair game.

"What is it with you two? Are you trying to harsh my mellow?" Keeping her eyes closed, Caitlin hoped Jessica would give up probing for information.

"Harsh your mellow?" Jessica laughed loudly.

"Pfft. All right. What do you want to know?" she asked.

"Just whatever you can tell us."

Caitlin reluctantly sat up. "A nineteen-year-old female died at a party, possibly from a combination of drugs and alcohol. We won't know for certain until the autopsy tomorrow. I was unable to obtain a search warrant today because the judges are away for the holidays. There is one due back tomorrow. That's all I can say for now."

"That's terrible."

"Natalie did the notification, and she said the family is shattered. I can't imagine their pain. My nana always said that a parent should never outlive a child."

"My mom had the same expression," Mike said. "I miss my folks, especially at this time of the year."

"When did you last celebrate Christmas with your parents?" Caitlin asked turning Mike's previous question back on him.

"The year before the pandemic," he said.

"Is that when you met this troublemaker?" Caitlin asked indicating Jessica.

"Sort of. We bumped into each other that summer. I had intended to come back to Canada, but I had a bit of money saved up and decided to stretch my holiday."

"Stretch your holiday?" Jessica burst out laughing. "Come on, Mike. You can tell a better story than that! You make it sound like a week or two, instead of several months."

"Shush!" Caitlin said to Jessica. "You had your chance. This is Mike's story."

Mike reached for the open bottle of wine and topped up both Caitlin and Jessica's glasses before refilling his.

"Easy," Caitlin said, "or I'll be sleeping on your couch tonight."

"You're always welcome to use the spare bedroom," he said.

"Thank you, but not tonight. I have to be in early to organize the team, and then I have a nine o'clock interview with a friend of the deceased and her lawyer," Caitlin said. "Now, quit stalling and tell me how you hooked up with Jessica."

He slowly smiled. "It took careful, long-term planning and stealth. She was uneasy around me at first. I just happened to be at several social events after we first met, so she could get used to seeing me around."

Jessica's cheeks flushed. "It wasn't just you Mike. Any guy that I didn't know made me uncomfortable."

Puzzled by Jessica's admission of unease, Caitlin bluntly asked, "Why?"

Mike looked at Jessica silently asking for approval to explain.

"Go ahead. Tell her."

"Did Jessica tell you about the drug lord, Alfonso Fuentes, who was obsessed with her?" he asked.

"She didn't, but I knew a little about it," Caitlin said.

"How?" Jessica asked. It was her turn to be puzzled. *How could Caitlin know about something that had happened in Mexico?*

"I'm an investigator, so…," Caitlin spread her hands like a magician. "I investigate. When you stuck your nose into Kingsley Quartermain's death, I called a retired cop friend. Coincidentally he and his wife had retired to the same little island where you lived."

"Who?"

"Calvin and Marie Adair."

"You mean Red? The guy with the curly white beard who doubles as Santa?"

"Yes, him."

"Well, hell. He never said he was a retired cop."

"That's not surprising. Most cops, retired or working, like their privacy."

"What did he tell you about me?" Jessica demanded.

"As it turns out, just the basics. He promised to email me the details, but then he forgot, and I was busy with the Quartermain case and it slipped my mind until now," Caitlin said. "However, I can always remind him that he promised me details." She said, then winked at Mike. "You were trying to tell me a story before this meddler butted in."

Mike continued with his story. "Fuentes took surreptitious photos of Jessica at Carlos and Yasmin's wedding. He figured out where she lived and broke in, stealing some of her lingerie. He returned a third time to Isla Mujeres and tracked her while she and Sparky were out in her golf cart. He forced her to drive him back to her house."

"Jesus," Caitlin muttered.

"Luckily for Jess, she spotted her island brother Diego Avalos and was able to signal that she desperately needed help. Diego along with Sergeant Ramirez, and a few others set up a rescue operation.

Ramirez shot the guy and Diego dashed inside to help Jessica.

"She had badly bruised ribs. Two black eyes. A wrenched neck." Mike leaned in and gently kissed the side of her head. "She was a goddamn mess when I met her."

"Don't forget Sparky's trauma," Jessica added. Hearing his name, Sparky sidled over and leaned against her leg, giving her a sad-eyed expression as if he knew exactly what they were talking about.

Mike motioned. "You tell the story."

"Fuentes made me secure Sparky with duct tape to prevent him from barking or attacking him." She smoothed his fur. "The poor little guy was so traumatized."

"But Sparky got even," Mike prompted her. When Jessica had eventually told him the story about Sparky and the dead cartel boss, he'd laughed until he was gasping for breath.

"Yes, he did. After Sergeant Ramirez killed Fuentes, Diego barged inside to rescue Sparky and me. He was able to cut a lot of the tape off Sparky, who then marched to the front door and pissed on Fuentes' corpse. Right on his face!"

The three of them collapsed in loud laughter eventually winding down to sputtered giggles.

Mike said, "No matter how many times I hear that part of the story, it's still bloody hilarious." He wiped his eyes, then continued. "Our first, brief, encounter was at Punta Sur a few days later. She looked like she'd gone a few rounds in a boxing ring and was as jumpy as hell. I was smitten."

Intrigued, Caitlin asked. "Why were you smitten? In my experience, those types of injuries usually indicate a domestic abuse situation. Why would you want to get involved?"

Mike grinned and wrapped his arm around Jessica, pulling her closer, "because she said, 'you should have seen the other guy' and I knew this woman was a fighter. A survivor. And I wanted to get to know her. To know her story."

A teasing grin played across her face. "But I didn't make it easy for you."

"No, I kept extending my stay to get to know her, but I was also supervising the construction of a new winery in Ontario, and I had to fly back and forth a few times."

"So, when did you ask her out?" Caitlin asked.

"Not until January 31st. Her golf cart had broken down, and I stopped and offered my mechanical expertise," Mike said.

"In his expert opinion, the chrome-reverse-sliding gear was broken on my golf cart," Jessica deadpanned.

"There's no such thing," Caitlin objected, then uncertainly asked. "Is there?"

"It doesn't exist," Jessica agreed.

"I didn't have a clue how to fix a golf cart, and I used it as an opportunity to chat with her. Then, I offered Jess and Sparky a ride home," he said. "In the meantime, she phoned her golf cart repair guy and very clearly told him where to find her cart, and who was giving her a ride. I'm surprised she didn't take a photo of me and send it to Sergeant Ramirez," he joked.

"It crossed my mind," Jessica replied, then turned to Caitlin. "My traitorous dog approved of Mike, so here we are."

"Nope! I'm not accepting the Coles Notes version," Caitlin said. "Keep talking."

"Our first date was interesting. We had two chaperones." Grinning, Mike held up two fingers. "She'd arranged for Carlos and Yasmin to coincidentally arrive at *Bally Hoo Restaurante* five minutes after we had ordered our drinks."

Caitlin tossed her head back, laughing. "Jessica, you didn't."

"I did. I still wasn't sure about him."

"And then there was the full-access package to the Island Time Music Festival that one of my pals had purchased and couldn't use," Mike said, making air quotes around the word pals.

"What does that mean?" Caitlin asked.

"The music festival is a big deal on the island," Jessica said. "It attracts musicians and songwriters from Nashville, and a massive crowd of country music fans to the island. Mike showed up at the *Loco Lobo Restaurante* where I worked as a waitress, and offered me the expensive four-day package, free, saying his friend couldn't use it and didn't want any money for the tickets. I was pretty sure Mike was making the whole thing up about his buddy and was trying to ask me out on a date, without actually asking me on a date."

"Did you go to the events with him?" Caitlin asked.

"Only one," Mike replied, his eyes crinkling with laughter.

"He sprung it on me. The restaurant was super busy because of the festival, and I could only get one day off out of the four. I let some of my co-workers attend the other events."

"Ouch. That was an expensive and misguided romantic gesture," Caitlin said.

"The only event that Jessica could attend was at Big Daddy's on the beach," Mike said, with a chuckle.

"Remember our sour-faced waitress?" Jessica asked.

"What are you talking about? She liked me," Mike said, innocently pointing at himself.

"She definitely wanted something more than just your drink order."

"And then what happened?" Caitlin asked impatiently.

"We had barely got our first drink when one of the warm-up musicians dropped dead on the stage," Jessica said.

"That's not what I thought you would say," Caitlin said.

"It was my first experience of Jessica inserting herself into a police investigation. Unasked." Mike said.

"I am very familiar with her tactics. That's how the three of us met at *No Regrets Winery*," Caitlin said, checking the time on her phone. "Dammit, it's late. I have to go. I want to hear the ending, but it will have to wait until next time."

"Are you sure you don't want to sleep here?" Jessica asked. "You can get up as early as you need. I'll probably be walking Sparky by six-thirty."

"No, my wretched cat will make my life a misery if I abandon her again," Caitlin reluctantly stood up and headed to the door. She pulled on her jacket and boots, then kissed Mike on the cheek, and hugged Jessica. "Thanks for a wonderful evening. And don't forget I want to hear more."

As soon as the front door closed, Mike reached for Jessica. "Come here you. We have some catching up to do," he said, smothering her response with his lips.

When their lips unlocked, Jessica quickly scanned the room. The candles were out. Most of the kitchen mess had been cleaned up. And the Franklin woodstove was safely banked for the night. "Race you to bed," she yelled and disappeared.

"What about Sparky? Doesn't he need a last walk?"

"Nope. We went out while you and Caitlin were loading the dishwasher. Leave him in the living room tonight."

Mike leaned down and rubbed Sparky's head. "Sorry, pup you heard the boss lady. We're gonna be doing adult stuff and you have to sleep out here tonight."

Slouching toward his second favorite bed, Sparky gave Mike a look that spoke of abandonment, starvation, and certain death at the hands of an axe-murderer.

"Don't be such a drama queen. You'll survive." He patted Sparky again and headed to the bedroom.

"Hurry up or I might fall asleep!"

Chapter 15

Penticton RCMP station

"Good morning. Everyone looks bright-eyed and ready to go. I want to thank all of you for giving up your statutory day off to help with this investigation," Caitlin said.

"I'm happy to be here," Ethan said, looking at his coworkers who nodded in agreement. "Anything to keep SCU, Serious Crime Unit, in Kelowna, from scooping our case."

"Time is running out," Caitlin said. "The good news is the approval for our search warrant arrived a few minutes ago."

"Do you think we need all four of us to execute the warrant?" Natalie asked.

"No, I have other tasks for you and Evan. Just give me a moment." Caitlin scanned the bullpen, looking for someone who didn't appear to be snowed under with reports. She pointed at a young guy, who was watching her with keen interest. "Hey, you. New guy. What's your name?"

"Austin. Constable Jacob Austin."

"Okay, Austin, I need someone to relieve the guard at the scene of a suspicious death. Grab your jacket and follow us."

"Yes, ma'am."

"Hit the men's room first," she warned him. "You can't access the toilet at the scene."

"Thanks," he said, giving her a thumbs up as he veered sharply to the right.

Caitlin turned to Natalie, "I'd like you to thoroughly investigate Lucas Bankole, and anyone else that you can find registered to that condo," she said spelling the name and reciting the address. "I already know he has one outstanding warrant, for possession for the purpose of trafficking, but dig deeper and see what else you can find. We need to locate his mother. Maybe her son is spending the holidays with her."

"On it," Natalie said as she logged into a computer.

"Has anyone interviewed the neighbors on that floor?" Ethan asked.

"The uniforms tried to, but because yesterday was Christmas Day, most of the residents were away. Probably celebrating with their families," Natalie replied.

"We need a list of the condo residents who weren't home. I'll ask Sarge if we can have a couple of uniforms to knock on doors today, on the floor above, and the one below too." Caitlin said. "Can I leave that with you as well, Natalie?

"Sure. I can handle that."

"If they have security cameras, we should check the video for people leaving in a hurry. People that fit the age range, and demographics," Evan added.

"Do we know if the condo complex has security cameras?" Natalie asked.

Caitlin said, "That's your job, Evan. Find out about the CCTV. If they have cameras we need a copy, and we need to know what time Sarah, Olivia, Hayley, and Noah arrived."

"Does anyone have a contact number for the condo council? Or the president of the council?" Evan asked.

Everyone shook their heads.

"Okay, I'll work on that," Evan said.

"Also ask the 911 dispatch for the ambulance callout time, then check the CCTV for a hurried exit of anyone else, around that time," Caitlin said.

"Got it."

"Ethan let's get going. We must be back here before nine, for a second interview with Olivia Caponera," Caitlin said.

Seated at his desk, Evan circled his arm over his head and called out, "mount up, and ride," a reference to the full name of the Royal Canadian Mounted Police.

Ethan Jones dropped his chin and eyed the younger constable. "That is worse than a dad-joke."

"And yet it's still my favorite," Evan said, with a cheeky laugh, as he began to search for the council members. "Good hunting, everyone."

Chapter 16

The condo complex

Caitlin, Ethan, and Jacob Austin headed to the main entrance of the condo tower where a man waited. Anxiously shifting from foot to foot, he demanded, "What is this all about? Has my tenant damaged the suite? Where is my tenant?"

"Good morning, sir. I assume you are Mr. Morgan?"

"Yes, yes. Of course, I am. Tell me please, what is going on?"

"We spoke on the phone. I am Corporal Caitlin Smith of the General Investigative Section of the Penticton RCMP," she said. "We don't know where your tenant is. We have legal authorization to search the unit and remove evidence pertaining to an incident," Caitlin handed him a copy of the search warrant.

"But why? What has happened?"

"As I explained sir, there has been a serious incident here. We need you to open the main doors and activate the elevator for us. We already have a key to the unit."

"The officer sitting outside my apartment wouldn't let me access my property," he complained. "How can I see if there is damage?"

"Yes sir, those are his orders. Please come with us and I'll explain."

As the elevator rose, Caitlin watched the floor numbers as people often do when enclosed in a small elevator with strangers, or in this case one stranger. When the doors opened, she stepped out and glanced at Morgan. "Which way, sir?"

"That way," he said, stabbing his finger to the right.

Snapping on disposable gloves, Caitlin greeted the constable perched on a folding chair in front of the door, "Hey, Matt, we've got it now. Thanks so much for volunteering for this."

"No problem. I can always use the overtime pay," Matt said. "Should I leave the chair or take it back to the station with me?"

"Leave it please, for Constable Austin," she said pointing at the man beside her, then turned to Ethan. "Do we know when FIS is arriving?" She asked referring to the Forensic Investigation Section of the RCMP.

His phone dinged with an incoming text. "They are at the front door and need someone to let them in."

"Mr. Morgan, we are going to need an elevator key fob for a few hours. May we have yours? I'll make sure it is returned to you as soon as we are finished here," Caitlin said.

"Not until you tell me what is going on!" Placing his fists on his hips, his dark complexion flushed with impatience.

"I understand sir, but for the moment, please let Constable Jones use your fob to bring our forensic people up to this floor," she said, firmly.

"Fine!" He ungraciously dropped his key fob into Ethan's outstretched hand. "Now tell me what happened here."

Caitlin motioned for him to lower his voice, then leaned closer. "A young woman died early on Christmas morning. She was here with friends, then she was rushed to the hospital by ambulance. We have to search for evidence and our forensic team will be doing several tests. In the meantime, no one, except an authorized police officer, may enter or remove anything from the unit. Do you understand, sir?"

"Died? Here? In my condo?" His voice squeaked with anxiety.

"Please keep your voice down, sir. She died on her way to the hospital."

"But where is Louis?"

Puzzled, Caitlin asked, "Louis? Do you mean your renter?"

"Yes, Louis Fortier. Where is he?" Morgan demanded.

"We don't know sir. There is a Canada-wide warrant out for the arrest of Lucas Bankole. Our information search shows him living at this address."

"No, that's not possible. My renter's name is Louis Fortier, and I did a background check on him. He is clean."

She grabbed her phone, found a previous booking photo of Lucas, and turned the screen toward Morgan. "Is this your renter?"

"Yes. Louis Fortier. As I keep telling you, he's clean. I checked."

"This person," she pointed at her phone, "goes by the name of Lucas Bankole, and he has an outstanding arrest warrant," Caitlin replied, switching to the notetaking function on her phone. "Spell the last name, Fortier, Mr. Morgan."

He did. It was the standard spelling for the common French-Canadian surname.

"And a phone number?"

Morgan consulted his phone and recited the number. "There is no use in calling him. He's not answering. I have tried several times this morning to ask him what happened here."

"If he does contact you, please give him my phone number. We need to speak to him," Caitlin pointed at the cell number on the business card that she offered him. "And who did your renter use for references?"

"His last two employers. I spoke to both of them and they said he was a good guy. Reliable. Steady worker."

"Do you remember the names?"

"I made a note in my phone. They were two different contractors in Surrey," he said, checking his phone and reciting the company names.

"And phone numbers?"

Morgan huffed. "Couldn't you just look them up on the internet?"

"It's quicker if you give me the numbers that you called, sir."

"Fine," he said, reciting the numbers.

"Did he pay his rent on time, Mr. Morgan?"

The man hesitated. "Most of the time. Recently I have had to remind him, but he is paid up to date."

"Any other complaints? Loud parties?"

One shoulder twitched, a tiny dismissive shrug. "Once or twice a neighbor has complained. It was nothing," he said.

Caitlin didn't agree but realized it was pointless to argue.

She tapped her phone and called the station, "Nat, it's me. Can you run a name for me? Louis Fortier. It's an alias for Lucas Bankole. And two construction companies in Surrey that either Fortier or Bankole used as references," she said reciting the information. "Yes, as soon as possible, please."

The elevator dinged softly, announcing the arrival of the forensic team. "I'm sorry Mr. Morgan. I have to ask you to leave. You cannot access this unit until we are finished and I give my approval."

"I will wait in the lobby until you are finished!" Morgan flung the words over his shoulder as he bustled angrily toward the elevator, nearly colliding with Ethan and the forensic technicians.

"I hope he has his toothbrush with him," Caitlin whispered as Ethan arrived beside her.

"And his pajamas," he added, quietly.

"Hello, and a belated Happy Holidays to all," Travis said, walking toward Caitlin.

"Same to you, Travis. I see you are dressed fashionably as always," she said, motioning at the white disposable bodysuits, encasing Travis and his assistant.

"The absolute latest in FIS fashion," he agreed. "What have we got?"

"A young woman overdosed in this unit. She was DOA at the hospital. The principal renter is unreachable. The owner is the gentleman who passed you in the hallway."

"He's not feeling the holiday spirit," Travis said.

"No, he's not."

"What are we searching for?"

"Drugs. Fingerprints. DNA. Signs of a struggle. The usual."

"Got it." Travis opened the door and began laying a pathway of heavy plastic stepping stones, to allow others to walk through the apartment with limited contamination of the floors.

A twenty-something technician followed, photographing everything. "Holy shit, there is a lot of expensive stuff in here," he muttered. "Multiple televisions, e-bikes, a kayak, gaming console. This is a freaking fantasy mancave."

"Concentrate, dude. Concentrate," Travis admonished, lightly.

"Yep. Just saying. I wanna live here." Bright flashes lit up the interior as the photographer zeroed in on items. He would take hundreds of photos, moving a few inches to the right with every image, until he had photographed the entire two-bedroom suite from every angle.

"Don't forget the deck," Caitlin said.

"Will do, although it doesn't look like it has been used in months," the photographer said. "The occupant appears to have lived mostly in the living area, and the bedrooms."

"Caitlin," Travis said as he reappeared beside her, "I found something you might be interested in."

"What?"

"There are signs of recent sexual activity in both bedrooms. I have taken samples."

"Interesting. According to a young woman that we interviewed yesterday there were three females and one male here at an impromptu party," Caitlin said. "I think the young lady left out a few details."

"And we are getting a lot of different fingerprints," Travis said. "It will take us a while to process everything."

"We expected that," Caitlin said. "The principal renter has a history of dealing drugs."

"Whoa, and what do we have here?" Ethan's voice came from the main bedroom.

"What's happening, Ethan?" Caitlin said, walking toward his voice. "Where are you?"

"I'm in the walk-in closet."

Caitlin joined him. "What did you find?"

With his gloved hands, Ethan tilted a large cardboard box so that Caitlin could look inside. "Someone, presumably Bankole, has a thriving business."

"A drug dealing business," Caitlin said.

"Yes, ma'am."

Chapter 17

Penticton RCMP station

Caitlin and Ethan were back in the interview room. They made a good team when interviewing suspects.

"Olivia," Caitlin said, as she placed the plastic evidence bag and the spare key on the table. "Just to confirm, this is the key that your friend Lucas Bankole gave you for his condo." For now, she held back the information of Bankole's outstanding warrant. McCarthy would try to use that information to paint Olivia as an innocent bystander, and Caitlin wasn't convinced that she was.

Olivia leaned forward and pretended to study the key. "That's the key, but I didn't know his last name was Bankole."

"Yes, Lucas Bankole. We were able to confirm that today," Caitlin said. "So, this is the key that you used to access his unit while he was away?"

"Yes, I've already said that. Lucas said I could come by and hang out there whenever I wanted to."

"Had you done that before?"

"No. It was my first time."

"December 24th was the first time that you were in his condo unit and he wasn't there?"

"Yes."

"Does Lucas have a roommate?" Caitlin asked.

"Maybe," Olivia's eyes fluttered to the side. "There is a lot of stuff in the apartment, but I never saw anyone else."

"How many times have you been in that unit when Lucas was there?"

"Why?" she asked, stalling for time to think of a good answer.

"Because I would like to know," Caitlin replied evenly.

"I...I don't remember."

"Take a guess. A dozen times? Ten times?"

"How is this relevant to your investigation, Corporal Smith?" McCarthy asked, his tone suggesting that her line of questioning was tedious and unrelated to the inquiry.

"I am trying to understand if Olivia is familiar with the building and Lucas's suite," she replied, briefly glancing at McCarthy. She noted his styled hair, upmarket suit, and monogrammed shirt cuffs. A little overdressed for her taste. McCarthy didn't meet her eye, instead, he doodled with his Montblanc pen on a leather-bound pad of paper, pretending to be unconcerned about her questions.

"If I had known I'd need an alibi, I would have kept track!" Olivia retorted. She'd heard that on a TV show. A suspect was being grilled by the police, and he shouted that perfect response to a stupid question.

Not responding to Olivia's snippy reply, Caitlin continued, "How did you access the building if Lucas wasn't home?"

"I used that key," she pointed at it, a tiny smirk playing at the corner of her mouth.

"And the elevator? How did you operate the elevator?"

"I pushed the button for his floor," she said. Now she smirked broadly at Caitlin, letting her know that was probably the stupidest question ever. "You know," she said, demonstrating with her right forefinger, "you just push the button, and the elevator goes to that floor."

"Except it doesn't."

"What do you mean?" Olivia shot a bewildered look at Ethan as if he was going to say, 'It's a joke, we were just kidding.'

"It doesn't go anywhere unless you have the electronic key fob," Caitlin explained.

"But..."

Leonard McCarthy interrupted again with his overly familiar question, "How is that relevant Corporal Smith?"

"Olivia is not telling the truth about how she accessed the building. An electronic fob is required to open any of the entrance doors, and to operate the elevator."

"I remember!" Olivia shouted. "There was another person ahead of us. She held the door open to let us in."

"And the elevator?"

"I showed her the key and said I had forgotten my fob. She pushed the button for my floor."

"Can you describe her?"

"Old. Like you. But with grey hair."

Ignoring the implied insult, Caitlin asked, "And what time was that?" While she and Ethan were executing the search warrant, Evan had obtained footage from the CCTV cameras. He was currently searching for images of Olivia and her friends arriving at the condo complex.

"I don't know. An hour or two before I called the ambulance."

"Can you be more precise?" Caitlin studied Olivia as the girl glanced at her fingers. She was probably calculating backward from one-thirty in the morning to a time that would fit with her storyline.

"I don't remember. It was later than ten o'clock, but not yet midnight, I guess."

"You don't remember what time you got to the condo?"

"Um, no. I wasn't paying attention."

"What time did Sarah pick you up?"

"I don't know."

"Perhaps Noah or Hayley will remember. My co-workers are interviewing them separately."

Instinctively, Olivia's fingers scrabbled fruitlessly for her phone, belatedly remembering she'd been forced to surrender it before the interview. *Oh God. They have to back me up! If they don't, I'll never speak to them again!*

Inwardly amused, Caitlin watched the panic flit across Olivia's face. "We have everyone's phones secured in lockboxes."

"I just thought I had lost it somewhere," Olivia lied. "This is very stressful for me, and it's making me forgetful."

"Yes, of course. Continuing on, what did you do while you are at Lucas's condo?"

"We watched TV."

"All of you watched TV?"

"Yes, all of us."

"What did you watch?"

"A movie on Netflix."

"And what movie was that?"

"A romantic comedy. I don't remember the name of it," Olivia answered. That was a safe guess because there was always a rom-com playing on Netflix.

"My wife and I like to watch rom-coms together," Ethan said. "Who were the actors? Maybe I can remember what movies they played in."

"What? Oh. Ryan whatshisname, and that blonde," she snapped her fingers, pretending to be searching her memory for names.

"Ryan Reynolds?" Ethan asked.

"Yeah. That's his name."

"The Proposal?" He suggested, knowing the lead was a dark-haired Sandra Bullock.

"Yes!" Olivia smiled gratefully at Ethan for helping her out. *He was hot, for an old guy.*

Ethan angled his notepad slightly toward Caitlin letting her read what he had written. *Wrong female lead, and that movie has already left Netflix.*

"Who suggested sampling the drugs that night?" She asked.

"We all did."

"Walk me through it, Olivia, everyone said all at once 'hey, let's sample his private stash'," she asked, a perplexed expression on her face.

"Yes, that's right."

"My goodness, that is an amazing coincidence, that everyone said the same thing at the same time."

"Well, maybe not exactly the same words or at exactly the same time, but we were all talking about it at the same time." *She and Hayley had begged Lucas for drugs, but surely Noah would back her up? Wouldn't he?*

"I see. Okay, let's talk about Sarah. Who gave her drugs?"

"No one. She took them herself," Olivia firmly stated.

"Have you ever seen Sarah use drugs before?"

"No. She must have taken too much. That's why she had a bad reaction and stopped breathing.

She didn't know how much to take." Olivia said eagerly searching for exoneration and compassion. "Right?"

"Where was Lucas while you were at his condo?" Caitlin said. A rapid change in questioning frequently brought better results.

Olivia's expression changed to confusion, "I don't know. I think he said he was going to spend Christmas with his mother."

"Where does his mother live? We would like to interview Lucas too," Caitlin held her pen over her notepad. She was certain the answer was going to be another, 'I don't know.'

Predictably Olivia answered, "I don't know."

It was time to get tougher. "Our forensic technicians found evidence of recent sexual activity in both bedrooms, and we are waiting on the DNA results from the semen," Caitlin said, focusing on Olivia's panicked expression. "Who else was in the condo, Olivia?" She didn't have any samples, except the renter Bankole, to compare to, and she wanted to shake Olivia up a little.

"Are you kidding me? That's gross," A deep flush rose on Olivia's face as her eyes darted around the room, refusing to settle on any of the adult faces staring back at her. *Who were they to judge her? Three dried-up oldies.* "I'm tired and got confused again. I meant to say, no one else was there."

"That's enough, Corporal Smith," Leonard McCarthy barked at Caitlin. "I need to confer with my client. She is stressed and needs a break."

In Caitlin's experience, anytime an experienced lawyer raised his or her voice to shout at the police officer, it typically meant that she'd struck a nerve. McCarthy had been caught off-guard, and he was annoyed.

Picking up on his cue, Olivia put one hand on her forehead, and let her shoulders slump. "Yes, I'm too exhausted to go on. This is a terrifying experience."

"Just two more easy questions," Caitlin said, "and then we'll consult with our colleagues who are interviewing Hayley and Noah."

Olivia shot another panicked look at McCarthy, "I want to go home," she said, whining like a pre-schooler.

He held up one hand, "A few more minutes and then we will leave." He stared at Caitlin. "I will allow two questions, and then we are done."

"Fine," Caitlin scanned her list of unasked questions, picking out two. "Olivia, who gave Sarah the drink?"

"What drink?"

"A glass of vodka and juice. Who gave it to her?" Caitlin asked.

"I have no idea. She must have mixed it herself...while I was watching the movie."

"What type of drugs did Sarah take?"

"I don't know. I couldn't see what she took from the dish."

"Was the dish on the counter when you arrived?" Caitlin asked, testing to see if McCarthy was keeping track of how many questions she'd asked.

"That's more than two questions. We're done here," McCarthy said.

And, yes, he was keeping track. "We'll finish this interview after Olivia has had some rest," Caitlin replied.

"At our convenience," McCarthy countered.

Caitlin waited until McCarthy led Olivia away, then turned to Ethan. "That was a pack of lies."

"Yep, I'm not sure anything was true, other than her name at the beginning of the interview."

"She panicked when I mentioned the semen samples."

"Totally freaked. I don't think she had thought of that," Ethan said.

"Any thoughts?"

"If Lucas Bankole was there that night, I would put money on Olivia and him hooking up, because she knew him. And maybe Hayley and Noah?" Ethan added, skeptically.

"Noah doesn't strike me as the kind of guy who would interest Hayley. I think she'd be more interested in the bad boys, like Lucas," Caitlin said.

"I suppose it's possible that Lucas had sex with both Olivia and Hayley," Ethan said. "Evan's checking the CCTV, and hopefully the quality is decent enough so that we can figure out how many people were there that night."

"Travis said he found multiple sets of prints in the unit. If Lucas is a dealer, who knows how many people were in and out of that unit," Caitlin said. "Anyway, let's see what's going on with Olivia's friends." She led the way to the viewing area, where they could listen and watch the other interrogations. Both rooms were dark and empty.

"What the hell? Where are they?"

Chapter 18

Penticton RCMP station

Walking swiftly to the office area, Caitlin called out, "Natalie?"

"Over here," she responded.

"Where are Hayley VanBeck and Noah Atkins? And their lawyers?"

"We questioned both Hayley and Noah separately but didn't get much out of either of them. We didn't want to interrupt your interview, so we checked with Sergeant Williams, and he said to let them go, for now. We can always recall them if something else comes up."

"Dammit. I wanted to see them. Watch their expressions, hear their voices."

"I'm sorry, Caitlin. I thought we were doing the right thing by checking with the sergeant," Natalie said, her face registering concern that perhaps she and Evan had made an error.

"It's fine. Sergeant Williams gave his approval," Caitlin said, brushing away Natalie's concern. "How did they respond to the question about the elevator fob?"

Natalie made a face, "Hayley didn't know anything about a fob. She thought Olivia pushed the button and the elevator went up."

"How about Noah?"

"Same thing," Evan answered. "He didn't know anything about a key fob. He answered the same as Hayley. Olivia pushed a button and the elevator went up."

"How did they respond when you mentioned the semen samples, and that we were waiting for DNA results?" Caitlin was eager to know their reactions.

Natalie stared at her, blank-faced. "What semen samples?" She turned to Evan, "Did you know about that?"

"No, nothing was mentioned in the file," he said. "I'm sorry Caitlin if we screwed up."

"Fricking hell." She slapped her hand on the desk. "Ethan and I were running late for our interview with Olivia, and I forgot to update the files. Totally my fault," she said. "Shit!"

"Don't worry, it's not a big problem, Caitlin. We can interview them again once we get the results," Ethan said.

"I know, but my mistake cost us time. Time that we don't have to solve this case," she said. "Sergeant Williams won't be able to fend off Serious Crimes Unit much longer."

After a moment, Evan Swan broke the glum silence. "Noah had an odd reaction during his interview," he said. "Noah started to say something about being invited as an afterthought, to make up the numbers, then he suddenly seemed afraid and clammed up."

"What do you mean?" Caitlin asked.

Evan flicked his head toward a monitor, "I'll show you on the video." He started the video, then fast-forwarded it to the approximate time, and let it run at normal speed. "Keep your eyes on him when he grumbles that he was only invited to make up the numbers."

"Stop!" Caitlin said. "Back it up and play that part again."

"Do you see what I mean?"

"Yes, he looks afraid. Like he just realized that he'd said something he wasn't supposed to say."

"I have a theory," Ethan Jones said.

"Let's hear it," Caitlin said.

"Your question on the whiteboard, 'how did they access the elevator without an electronic fob?' I think someone from the unit let them in. I don't know if it was the principal renter, Lucas, or someone else. I also think that when someone discovered that Sarah was in trouble, everyone cleared out, and he, meaning Lucas or someone who was staying in the condo, warned everyone not to say anything."

Caitlin studied Ethan. "Just to play Devil's Advocate, tell me how you came up with your theory."

"FIS found many sets of fingerprints in the suite. It seems Lucas likes to party, with friends, or maybe his customers. I think that one, or more, guests were in his suite on Christmas Eve."

"You don't think Lucas wanted all three for himself?"

"I think they were too young to agree to group sex, but," he shrugged, "maybe I'm wrong. Young women are a lot more advanced than when I was that age."

"What about what Noah said? He was invited to make up the numbers. That sounds like there was one other male in the unit, the source of the semen in the second bedroom," Caitlin said.

"That's more likely. I checked the closets in both bedrooms and they were jammed with clothing in two distinct styles indicating at least two adult males lived there. Both bathrooms were fully equipped with the normal toiletries for men. Different products and different scents indicating two men lived there. What I didn't see, was anything to indicate a female resident," Ethan said.

"I agree. And to prove, or disprove, that theory we have to find out just how many people were in that suite on Christmas Eve, and then identify and track them down," Caitlin said. "Any luck, Evan, with arrival times for our group?"

"I was just about to update you," he said. "The group arrived at eleven-fifteen on Christmas Eve."

"That's great! What about unexpected departures around the time that the ambulance arrived?"

"I had to stop searching while we interviewed Noah and Hayley," he said. "I'll get on it right now."

"Okay, text me as soon as you find something." She checked the time. "Right now, I have to attend Sarah's autopsy."

Chapter 19

Penticton Morgue

Caitlin held Sarah's phone over her face to unlock the screen and revealed the unfinished message to her mother.

...please call me. I need...

"What did you need Sarah? Why were you texting your mom? And why didn't you hit send?" Caitlin quietly asked the dead girl.

"Were you speaking to me?" Doctor Elizabeth Kennedy asked from the other side of the autopsy suite. Her short grey hair was hidden under her white cap, and intelligent eyes peered at Caitlin over the top of her mask.

"No, I was talking to Sarah. I asked her why there is an unsent text to her mother, asking her mom to call her."

Dr. Liz, pulled off her bloodstained gloves, inverting them and tossing them in the designated trash receptacle. "I have some experience with teenagers. They typically don't want their friends to know when they are uncomfortable with a situation and will often secretively text a parent to come and bail them out. To demand they come home, immediately, so that the teenager can convincingly moan and groan about their annoying,

116

overprotective parents." She snapped on a fresh pair of gloves and walked to the autopsy table.

"I didn't know you had kids," Caitlin said. "You've never mentioned them."

"I don't. I am the cool auntie to a brood of nieces and nephews. I'm the person who gets the middle of the night phone calls and texts, begging me to rescue them." Dr. Liz peered at the unsent message. "And that message is a call for help."

"The outcome might have been different if she had sent it."

"One of her friends might have noticed what Sarah was texting and badgered her to abandon the text. Peer pressure is difficult to withstand."

Caitlin nodded. "Yes, it is," she replied, thinking of her younger self refusing to give in to pressure to smoke cigarettes. She couldn't stand the smell that clung to her friends and her home was firmly off-limits to smokers, of any type.

Dr. Liz, continued, "I need the lab results, but I am quite confident that Dr. Atwal, the attending physician at the hospital was correct in her assessment. Sarah died from an overdose of alcohol and drugs, compounded by her low tolerance to both products."

"Can you tell me what type of drug?"

"Not definitively until I read the report, but judging by her reaction it would have been a depressant, perhaps a benzodiazepine. Something like Ativan."

"We found a bottle of Ativan at the condo. It's being processed for fingerprints."

Dr. Liz nodded. "Typically, it's used as an antianxiety medication to lower stress. It can also depress the heartbeat and breathing. Combined with alcohol, benzodiazepines can lead to unconsciousness or death."

"Any sign of recent sexual activity? We found semen in both beds."

Dr. Liz shook her head. "She's intact. She's never had sex recently or otherwise."

"Such a waste of a young life," Caitlin said, gently touching Sarah's hand again.

"It's a tragic waste," Dr. Liz said, then asked, "Did anything else of interest turn up at the scene?"

"A dish with an assortment of various prescription drugs. Likely the same dish that the group sampled. We also located a substantial amount of other restricted drugs. What appears to be Fentanyl, Ecstasy, and cocaine. We don't have confirmation yet, because the lab is closed for the holidays."

"Yes, it's a difficult time of the year to accomplish anything," the doctor agreed.

Caitlin cocked her head. "Why are you working? You are senior enough to be off for the entire week between Christmas and New Year's Day."

"Your boss, Sergeant Williams, and I go way back. He explained how the SCU hot shots are sniffing around your case, and he inspired me to do Sarah's autopsy today," Dr. Liz replied.

"Inspired?"

"He promised me a case of my favorite wine, *Adega Cabernet Sauvignon*."

"Sarge bribed you?" Caitlin asked, amused.

"I said inspired." The corners of her eyes crinkled in laughter.

"By the way," Caitlin pointed to the unobtrusive speakers. "This is an interesting choice for your music today."

"I select age-appropriate tunes when I have a new arrival and Taylor Swift seemed like a good fit for Sarah."

"I'm sure she appreciates your thoughtfulness," Caitlin said, and meant it. *Maybe Sarah could hear the music.* Caitlin did not believe in the standard church dogma but had recently decided that perhaps there was something unknowable in the unimaginably massive ocean of universes called the multiverse. Or as she thought of it, Out There.

"Do you have time for a cup of my superior coffee?" Dr. Liz asked, breaking into her thoughts.

"Not this time. Rain check?"

"You're welcome to visit anytime, preferably without bringing me another young guest," she said, gesturing to Sarah's body.

"Deal," Caitlin agreed. "Give Gerrard a hug from me."

"Will do. He's been asking when you are going to join us for another wine tasting."

She shrugged lightly, "No idea, but don't cross me off your list just yet." She pulled off the disposable protective gear and dumped it in the corresponding waste bins.

Dr. Liz lifted one hand in a brief wave, "No worries. We'll keep trying."

The pathologist studied Caitlin as she walked away. A forty-something, divorced doctor had recently moved into town. The new arrival, Jason Gregory, was tall like Caitlin, decent-looking, and had a wicked sense of humor. Maybe we should invite them over for dinner? With a handful of extra people, so that it wouldn't be an obvious setup. She sent her husband a brief text.

Caitlin says hi. Let's have a dinner party. Invite her and J Gregory.

Gerrard Kennedy replied. *Don't meddle. Love U.*

Dr. Liz snorted a laugh and replied. *Caitlin needs fun. Working on it now. XOXO.*

Chapter 20

Cactus Brewing

Olivia wiped down a table, preparing it for the woman who waited at the entrance. "Just for one?" she asked. Her stomach ached, and her head hurt. She had intended to book off sick after the interview at the police station, but her mother had insisted that going to work was the best way to keep her mind occupied. *I don't want to be here.*

"No, my friend will be joining me in a few minutes," the woman answered, letting her eyes roam over the other diners. Christmas carols trickled through the overhead speakers in the taproom. The restaurant was busy with clusters of customers, people looking for a casual meal in the gap between Christmas Day celebrations and New Year's Eve parties.

Olivia pointed at the chalkboard hanging above the bar. "When you've decided, just place your food and drink order at the bar," she said. "The bartender will give you the drinks, and I'll bring your food when it's ready." If she had to be at work today, it wasn't completely unbearable. Fewer bosses. Less scrutiny.

This time of the year was when most of the administrative staff took a few days off to be with their families. Even Rhys, the head brewer, was away until tomorrow and the brewhouse was eerily quiet. On a typical day, the kettle roared as the heat boiled the liquid. When geeky Noah had self-importantly tried to explain to her how the beers were made, she'd tuned him out, but the funny name for the smelly brown liquid stuck in her head. *Wort. Something like that. And that thing the brewers used to filter the beer created a loud thumping noise. A centrifuge? Don't remember. Don't care. Just happy I don't work on the grungy jobs, like Noah.*

"Thank you, I've been here a few times," Jessica replied pulling Olivia's attention back to her work.

"Okay, good," Olivia replied, smiling broadly like a cheerleader at tryouts. *Whatever. Just leave me a decent tip.*

Recognizing the hospitality manager, Mark Gifford, Jessica greeted him, "Hi Mark. Good to see you."

"Hi Jess, Merry Christmas," Mark replied. "What can I get you?"

"A pint of something hoppy, please." She glanced up at the chalkboard menu, happy to see her favorite tacos were still on the menu. Made with corn tortillas, salsa, shredded pork, and so many other delicious flavors it prompted a nostalgic memory of her other home, Isla Mujeres, Mexico.

"Our IPA is a good choice."

"That's perfect," she said.

"Hey Jess," a voice called from the front entrance.

"Caitlin, just in time. What can I get you?"

"The newest creation."

Jessica turned to Mark. "Newest?"

"Sure, our brewing team likes to create new choices all the time."

"Okay, a pint of whatever that is."

Jessica ferried the drinks to the table, and placed one in front of Caitlin, before setting hers on the table. "I'm glad you could make it," she said.

"Me too. Today is supposed to be my day off, but I've had a super busy morning, and I am starving."

"I remember you said you had an interview this morning."

"Yes. Before that, we searched and processed the condo." Leaning toward Jessica, she spoke quietly. "And then I attended the autopsy."

"That's a full day's work and it's only mid-afternoon," Jessica said.

"We're always shorthanded during the holidays, and I'm single with only my cranky cat waiting at home."

"You can actually eat food after attending an autopsy?"

"It's not ideal, but over time I've learned to cope," Caitlin said.

"Am I ever going to meet your cranky cat?" Jessica asked, changing their conversation to something more palatable.

"Sure. You are welcome to pop over anytime for a drink, or a cup of coffee. I can probably rustle up a few stale crackers and some moldy cheese."

"That sounds so enticing," Jessica replied.

Olivia casually glanced at the new arrival. Her voice sounded familiar. "Oh shit," she muttered. "It's that cop." She darted over to the serving station and nudged Hayley. "That nasty cop who questioned me this morning is here. Watch what you say."

Hayley craned her head, "I don't see a cop."

"The tall redhead at table six, sitting with the blonde."

"She's not in uniform."

"For God's sake, Hayley. She's a detective or something like that. She doesn't wear a uniform."

"Oh okay. That's your section so I don't have to worry."

"Can you deal with them, please?" Olivia whined. "She hasn't met you yet and I'm still too upset after she grilled me this morning."

Hayley studied Olivia's face. "Don't be such a baby. I was also *grilled* by the cops this morning."

"Not like me! They asked who I had sex with. It was humiliating."

"What? They didn't ask me that," Hayley said. "What did you tell them?"

"Nothing. I pretended I was exhausted, and my lawyer stopped the questioning."

"That's gross. Why would a cop ask that?"

"She said the science geeks found stuff in the beds," she said. The word semen made her lovemaking with Lucas, sound crude and disgusting. "Please, don't make me wait on that table."

"Fine, I'll do it, but if she's a cheap tipper you'll owe me."

"Sure," Olivia said. "Back in ten, I need a quick break."

"Not now, Livy it's super busy."

"Stop whining. I won't be long."

"Don't be such a bitch, Olivia," Hayley whispered fiercely.

"Same to you." Olivia stomped away into the brewery. Now Hayley knew she wasn't sick, just freaked out by the appearance of the cop. She couldn't book off and leave.

Olivia walked outside to have a quick smoke to settle her nerves, then keep busy until the cop and her friend left. She didn't smoke often. Cigarettes didn't do enough for her, but smoking weed at work was a sure way to get fired. She needed this job, in case things went sideways at home. Kent was making noises that she should move out on her own, to be more independent, and the thought of being forced to support herself made her want to puke. If she had to be nicer to him, then she'd suck it up, and do it.

Dropping her cigarette butt onto the pavement, Olivia ground it out with the toe of her shoe and re-entered the brewery. To avoid the cop and her friend in the main taproom, she ducked behind a tall stack of pallets holding thousands of new cans waiting to be filled. Curious the two women were discussing Sarah's death, she wished she had told Hayley to eavesdrop on their conversation.

Wasting time, Olivia idly studied the colorful, printed labels. A loud grinding noise caught her attention. She turned her head toward the noise and screamed.

Chapter 21

Cactus Brewing

In the taproom, Caitlin heard a high-pitched scream coming from the production area of the brewery, followed by the sound of something heavy banging into other objects. Then a shower of flimsy metal objects rattled across the hard floor.

She jumped to her feet, shooting a look toward the brewhouse. "Stay here. I'll be right back," she said to Jessica.

Jessica quietly huffed. "Not bloody likely." She followed a few steps behind. There was no way she was going to stay sitting at her table, pretending to enjoy her lunch while Caitlin dealt with whatever was happening in the brewhouse.

A babble of shocked exclamations and concerned questions swept through the taproom, as some customers half-rose from their chairs, intending to investigate the noise.

"I'm a police officer." Pulling her official identification out of her pocket, Caitlin held it high for others to see. "Everyone, please remain seated."

Caitlin quickly approached the dark-haired man who stood uncertainly beside the bar, "Corporal Smith," she said, displaying her badge again. "Who is the duty manager?"

"It's me, Mark Gifford. Until later, then Piper or Sean will be in," he said.

"Piper and Sean are owners, right?"

"Co-owners, with Reid and Rhys. One or the other is usually here," Mark said. "What do you need me to do?"

"Call them if I give you a wave from the back. Understand?"

"Should I come with you?" Mark asked.

"No, please stay here and keep everyone out of the back area," Caitlin said.

Mark nodded. "Okay." As Caitlin walked into the brewhouse, Mark turned to the cluster of worried faces that had appeared from the kitchen. "Is everyone okay?"

Tyler, the head chef did a quick count. "Yep, we're all fine. Who screamed?"

"That's what I'm trying to find out. Hayley are you, and Olivia, okay?" Mark walked closer so that Hayley could hear him over the rising chatter of nervous voices.

Frozen in place beside a table, Hayley swept her eyes across the taproom, then back to Mark. "Olivia's not here. She said she wasn't feeling well and went outside for a smoke."

"We need to find her, right now," Mark said.

"I don't know where she is," Hayley replied, her voice quavering. "And what about Dylan? Where is he?"

"Right. He's working today," Mark said. "I'll look for him."

Overhearing their conversation, Jessica said, "Mark, are you missing two employees?"

"Yeah, Olivia Caponera and Dylan Hughes. She's a waitress in the taproom, and Dylan is an assistant brewer. He should be in the back somewhere."

"I thought the brewhouse was shut down for the holidays?" Jessica asked.

"Yes, but someone has to check on the brews regularly. Rhys and his assistants share those duties."

"Okay, I'll tell Corporal Smith that there are two employees unaccounted for," she said, walking quickly toward the entrance to the brewhouse.

"Caitlin, no one has seen Olivia or the assistant brewer, Dylan Hughes."

"Olivia Caponera? I didn't see her here."

"According to the other waitress, she popped outside for a cigarette."

"Okay. Look outside. Maybe Olivia and Dylan are having a cigarette break together. I need to take a closer look at this," Caitlin said, pointing to the heap of rubble.

She studied the hundreds or perhaps thousands of empty cans on the floor. Some were still contained in the plastic wrap surrounding each pallet of cans, others had broken free with the force of hitting the concrete and were scattered across the expanse of the brewhouse. She warily eyed the

129

other stacks, wondering what had caused the collapse.

"What a mess," Jessica said, as she opened the back door, and stepped outside. "Olivia Caponera? Dylan Hughes? Are you here?" She walked up and down the alley, from one end of the brewery to the other, calling their names.

Caitlin slowly picked her way through the aluminum rubble, watching for any sign of whoever had screamed. "Olivia? Dylan? Can you hear me? I need to account for everyone."

Jessica re-entered the brewery. "There is no one out there. Do you think someone is under there?"

"It's a good possibility," Caitlin responded. "We'll need assistance to find out," she said pointing at the pile of rubble.

"Sparky is outside in my car. I'll bring him in for a quick sniff."

"He's not properly trained to find people."

"And yet he does."

"Fine. Get him."

Jessica scooted out the back door and ran to her car parked at the front of the building. She unlocked the car door, attached Sparky's leash, and gave it a gentle tug, "Come on pooch. We have work to do."

She walked as quickly as his short legs could manage to the rear door. Dogs weren't allowed inside the brewery and there was no sense in parading him through the taproom in front of the other guests. "Okay pooch, show Caitlin what you can do," she said, unleashing him.

"Doesn't he need something to smell, like a piece of clothing?" Caitlin asked.

"It's better if he does, but he instinctively knows to find people who are in trouble," she said. "Buscar, Sparky. Buscar."

Caitlin cocked an eyebrow at her.

"You know Spanish is his first language," Jessica said while keeping an eye on her dog as his nose skimmed the floor vacuuming up the interesting scents.

"He still understands it?"

"A little. But we are both forgetting the words," Jessica replied. "Come on little man, let's do this."

Sparky plowed his way through the belly-deep aluminum cans, moving toward the deepest pile of rubble. His tail spun in excited circles as he neared the toppled wooden pallets. He turned his head to look at Jessica and barked, once.

"Sparky. Wait. You're getting too close," she cautiously reached over and clipped on his leash. "I think someone is under there," Jessica said to Caitlin.

Walking a short distance away, Caitlin tapped 9-1-1, on her phone. She crisply reported her name, rank, location, and nature of the problem, requesting both the fire department to help with removing the rubble, and the ambulance to care for any potential victims. Disconnecting the call, she said, "We have to keep back in case one of the other stacks collapses. You should stand by the back door. Keep anyone else from entering. I'll update Mark so that he can inform the owners and I'll block the other entrance," she said, walking toward the taproom.

Jessica moved Sparky back and gave him an enthusiastic butt scratch. "Good boy. Such a good, good boy," she praised him for his actions, hoping that he had made a mistake, and there wasn't an injured person buried under the rubble. Waiting for help to arrive, she studied the remaining columns of pallets and cans. They looked stable. *What caused one to topple over?*

"Hey, who are you and what's going on?" A young male voice asked.

Jessica spun around. A dark-haired twenty-something guy stood beside her with a confused expression on his face.

"Are you Dylan Hughes?"

"Yeah. What the heck happened here?" He pointed at the mess.

"There was an accident and we've been searching for you and Olivia Caponera. Have you seen her?"

"She was having a smoke out by the garbage bins a few minutes ago."

"Why didn't you hear the noise? It was really loud," Jessica asked.

"I was in the coolers, checking on the brews. It's soundproof, and I was listening to tunes on my EarPods," he said, pointing at his left ear.

"Damn, I didn't think to look in there for you," Jessica said. "And you didn't hear anything?"

"Nope."

"I'm glad you are okay," Jessica said. "Corporal Smith is in the taproom. Could you let her know that you're safe? Tall red-haired, wearing street clothes, not a uniform. You'll know when you see her," she added with a half smile.

He shrugged. "Sure. But shouldn't I be guarding this instead of you?"

Jessica pointed at Sparky. "I can't take him into the restaurant."

"Got it."

Chapter 22

Cactus Brewing

"We're sorry but we are closing the taproom. Lunch is on us today," Sean Dawson said turning the Open sign to Closed, as he apologized for interrupted lunches that were being efficiently packaged into takeaway boxes. The owners, Piper, Reid, and Sean had arrived quickly after Mark's phone call alerting them to a problem at the brewery.

"What happened, Sean?" A customer asked.

"Why are the fire and ambulance here?"

"Was someone hurt?"

Sean smiled reassuringly at the group and held up his hands. "Honestly, I don't know exactly what happened. We were told to shut the brewery," he said, skipping any details.

Constable Natalie Garcha stood at the front door, holding a clipboard. Ethan Jones, Evan Swan, and Natalie had answered Caitlin's call for backup. "Before you go, please print your names and phone numbers on this list."

"Why?" one man demanded.

"It's just a precaution, sir. In case we have any questions later on," Natalie explained. If someone was injured or dead under the pile of pallets, the coroner and FIS would be called to gather evidence, and the employees and patrons would have to be interviewed.

A few minutes after the 9-1-1 call, the fire and ambulance crews had entered through the warehouse delivery entrance. While the firefighters worked on stabilizing the rubble so that they could search where Sparky was indicating, the ambulance attendants waited with their equipment.

"Hayley, are you certain Olivia said that she was going outside for a cigarette? I didn't know she smoked," Piper Dawson said.

"She occasionally does, and she said…um…that she wasn't feeling well," Hayley avoided Piper's eyes.

"Hayley, please tell me the truth," Piper asked. "I'd be relieved, not angry if she left early."

"I don't know if she left, but I know she was avoiding her," she said indicating Caitlin.

"Avoiding Corporal Smith? Why?"

Caitlin turned at the mention of her name, "Hayley, why was Olivia avoiding me?"

"You upset her."

"Being interviewed can be stressful," Caitlin admitted. "Do you think she went home?"

Hayley shrugged and looked away. "If she did, she didn't tell me."

Caitlin swung her eyes back to the pile of rubble, hoping the young woman had skipped out early, and wasn't buried under the pallets and cans.

Ethan walked over to stand beside her. "What does your gut tell you?" he quietly asked.

She nodded toward Sparky. "Jessica thinks Sparky can smell someone under the pile. He might be mistaken, but I called for assistance in case he's right."

"Sparky is usually right," Ethan said.

"I know, but this time I hope he's wrong," Caitlin said.

"Captain, I've got something," a young fireman yelled. He was crouched with one hand buried under loose cans, "I can feel a foot and an ankle."

"Can you find a pulse on the ankle?"

The firefighter slowly moved his hand further under the pile, and sat motionless for a minute. "Yes! There is a weak pulse," he said.

"Okay, crew, let's get that person out," the captain motioned for several firefighters to support the pallets, while two firefighters and the two ambulance attendants slowly uncovered the person.

"We have a female," one shouted, as a woman's shoe and ankle came into view.

"Dammit," Caitlin sighed. "It could be Olivia."

A few minutes later, Olivia's face was uncovered. One ambulance attendant checked her respirations and pulse, then settled an oxygen mask over her mouth and nose. "We need to transport her, ASAP."

Caitlin turned to Ethan. "Can you start interviewing the kitchen staff? I'll speak to Mark and Hayley."

"What about the other guy, Dylan?"

"Definitely. Either you or me, depending on who is available first."

Chapter 23

Cactus Brewing

Standing near the delivery door, Jessica kept Sparky off to one side. She didn't want the health department penalizing the brewery for allowing a dog inside, but her curiosity itched at her. How could one heavy stack just topple over? The others appeared to be stable. She slowly guided Sparky along the outside wall, toward the spot where Olivia had been found.

Whispering to Sparky, "Buscar, search," she led him deeper into the room. "Do you smell anything pooch? Sorry, that was a stupid question. Your supersensitive nose obviously smells something. Lots of somethings," she said conversationally to her dog as if he knew exactly what she was saying.

His tail up and nose closely skimming the cement floor, Sparky inhaled noisy, deep breaths and ignored Jessica's prattling questions. He was in the zone. His aging, arthritic body vibrated with each lungful.

"Who are you talking to, Jess?"

She twitched, "Ethan, I didn't know you were close enough to hear me."

"Yep. I assume you were asking Sparky for his opinion?"

"Yes, I was," she said.

"Does he know whodunnit?" Ethan asked.

"That's a first. You admitting that Sparky might help solve your case."

"Nah, I know he's smart. I just didn't want to admit that he might be smarter than me. Any intel you have to share would be appreciated."

"I don't know anything yet, but I am curious why just one of the stacks suddenly toppled over." She pointed to the remaining columns.

"Me too. That's why I'm poking around back here," Ethan said. He squatted and pointed at three deep gouges in the concrete. "That's odd. It looks as if the entire column was shoved," he tapped his phone calling Caitlin.

"Yes?"

"Is there a photographer on the scene?"

"Not yet. Why?"

"Come to where Olivia was buried. Jess and I might have found something," Ethan said.

"I thought you were questioning the staff?"

"That's almost finished. Natalie and Evan are with the last two," he said. "I need to show you something interesting."

"On my way," she said and swiftly walked to join Jessica and Ethan. "Did anything unusual surface when you questioned the employees?"

"Not really. Except there is no way to confirm Dylan's statement that he was working in the cooler with his EarPods and he didn't hear the noise."

"So, we'll keep him on our list for now," she said. "What did you want to show me?"

Ethan pointed at the gouged concrete. "Those scratches match the three crosspieces that support each pallet. It looks like this stack was forcefully moved."

Imitating Ethan's earlier action, she squatted and examined the marks. "Yes, it does. Find out the ETA of the photographer," she said snapping several images with her phone.

"Will do," Ethan replied.

Caitlin's original conclusion, that Olivia's accident was an unfortunate mishap, was edging toward the possibility that it was a deliberate act. *If it's deliberate, what was the motive? Anger aimed at Olivia? Reckless vandalism?*

"Why are you and Sparky hanging around and contaminating my scene?" Caitlin asked Jessica.

"Sorry, I was curious. I brought Sparky over to sniff the area hoping he could find something."

"Anything?"

"Nothing other than the scratches that Ethan noticed."

Caitlin rolled her aching shoulders, and cooly examined her friend. "Let him poke around a bit more. Be careful. Don't knock anything over."

"Okay." Jessica tugged lightly on Sparky's leash, "Buscar, search."

"I bet we are the only Canadian police force that has a furry bilingual detective," Caitlin murmured as she watched Sparky minutely examine every surface.

"He's unique and thorough," Ethan chipped in, adding, "Our photographer should be here in ten."

"Good. Do you have any theories on what happened here?"

"Well, my first thought was an accident, but now, I think this might have been a targeted attack."

"Me too. Who do you think the target was?"

"My first thought is Olivia. She's not well-liked."

Interested, Caitlin turned to look at him. "Where did you get that from?"

"Several of her workmates have strong opinions on Olivia. In their words, she has a snotty attitude."

"About what?"

"Everything. Her coworkers. The job. The owners. The brewery. Her parents. Previous school friends." He shrugged. "Everything."

"Is she disliked so much that someone would attempt to kill her?" She asked.

"Maybe it was an impulsive act. Maybe the culprit didn't think about the consequences."

Jessica and Sparky came into view again. She beckoned to Caitlin and Ethan, "Did you see this?"

"What?" Caitlin strode toward her.

"That forklift is badly parked. I think someone used it, possibly to shove the stacks, then quickly abandoned it."

Caitlin lifted her eyebrows, "And how do you deduce that, Sherlock?"

"Mike and I work with forklifts at the winery. No one parks the vehicle with the tines partially raised. It's dangerous," Jessica said, pointing to the metal extensions that were raised and aimed waist-height. "The correct way to park a forklift is to set the handbrake, lower the tines completely, then slightly tilt the mast forward until the tips are touching the ground to prevent impalement or tripping accidents."

"Huh. I didn't know that," Caitlin said. "Did you touch the forklift?"

"No, I just looked to see if the keys were in the ignition, and they are."

"Is that normal?"

"It's not unusual, especially if more than one person is certified to operate the forklift."

"I'm curious, are you certified?" Ethan asked.

Jessica met his eyes. "Driving the forklift isn't my job."

He grinned. "You're side-stepping my question Ms. Sanderson."

Caitlin chuckled and held up her hand. "Let it go, Ethan. She's not under suspicion. This time."

"What do you mean, this time? When have I ever been under suspicion?" Jessica snorted.

"Would you like me to list all of the occasions when I wanted to arrest you for interfering in a police investigation?"

"That's different. That's just me being helpful, and you being ungrateful."

"You win." Caitlin tossed her hands up, in surrender. "I've got to update the boss," she said, tapping her phone to call Sergeant Williams.

Chapter 24

Penticton Regional Hospital

Caitlin and Ethan stood in the hallway of the emergency ward, waiting for the attending physician to update them on Olivia's condition. It was noisier and busier than the night when she had tried to question Olivia about Sarah's overdose.

Workers in scrubs swirled around the central desk, updating the electronic charts, answering the unending phone calls, and pushing equipment carts for blood tests and EKGs in and out of curtained cubicles.

"Constable Smith!" Stephanie Ferguson had arrived, shouting along the corridor to Caitlin.

"Hello Mrs. Ferguson," Caitlin replied calmly, "and it's Corporal Smith, not Constable."

"Have you arrested the animal who injured my daughter?"

"No, Mrs. Ferguson. We are waiting for the doctor's permission to speak to Olivia."

"The doctor's permission? You need my permission, not his."

"Mrs. Ferguson, your daughter is an adult," Caitlin replied evenly. "We only need the doctor's permission to ask Olivia a few questions about what happened."

"That's ridiculous! I'm calling our lawyer."

"Your choice," Caitlin replied, then turned toward the doctor as she exited Olivia's cubicle. "Dr. Atwal, we've met before. I'm Corporal Caitlin Smith, and this is Constable Ethan Jones."

"Yes, of course, I remember you, and it's a pleasure to meet you, Constable Jones."

"May we speak to Olivia Caponera for a few minutes?"

The doctor glanced at Stephanie and then back to Caitlin. "Yes, she is awake and stable. Please keep your visit brief. We will be sending her for X-rays shortly."

"X-rays? Why? I'm her mother and I need to see my baby girl, first before the police."

Dr. Atwal motioned for Stephanie to remain calm. "Mrs. Caponera please let the officers ask their questions and then we'll let you see her before we do more tests."

"It's Ferguson. Stephanie Ferguson. I remarried."

"My apologies Mrs. Ferguson. Please give the officers a few minutes with Olivia," Dr. Atwal said, as Caitlin and Ethan entered the cubicle, leaving her to deal with Stephanie Ferguson.

"Fine. Now give me an update on my daughter."

"Olivia is an adult and I need her permission to divulge her medical information," Dr. Atwal hedged.

During the examination, Dr. Atwal discovered that Olivia was two months pregnant. Satisfied that the fetus was still viable and hadn't spontaneously aborted when Olivia was injured, she asked the young woman if she was aware of her condition. Olivia had adamantly denied that she was pregnant because she was using a contraceptive. Atwal persisted and finally convinced Olivia that she was indeed pregnant. The shocked young woman begged her not to tell her mother. Atwal had then instructed Olivia to eat well, get plenty of sleep, get regular medical checkups, and more importantly not drink alcohol, smoke tobacco, or use recreational drugs. Her stern message seemed to float unheard past Olivia's ears as she blathered on about someone trying to kill her.

"Now, if you will excuse me," Dr. Atwal said, to Stephanie Ferguson, "I have other patients waiting."

"How rude," Stephanie said to the doctor's back.

Dr. Atwal's neutral expression hid her frustration, then as she entered the adjacent cubicle, she smiled warmly at the man lying in the bed. "Hello there. And what do we have going on with you?" As she began her examination, she could hear Corporal Smith speaking quietly to Olivia. Presumably asking her what had happened.

"Do you remember anything, Olivia? Was anyone working nearby? Did you hear any unusual noises? Any information would help us," Caitlin said.

146

"I don't remember anything." She gingerly touched the bandage covering her head. "I have a head injury, and a broken arm."

"I'm sorry you are in pain, but we are hoping you can give us more information so that we can figure out what happened. Let's start with what you can remember. Where were you standing when you were outside?"

"What's that got to do with someone trying to kill me?"

Caitlin blinked. "Why do you think someone tried to kill you?"

"Those stacks have never fallen over before."

"Alright. But it could help you remember more details if we start at the beginning. So, where were you standing outside?"

"I walked away from the building. I was over by the dumpsters."

"That's quite a distance from the door. Why so far?"

"It's against the law to smoke close to an entrance. You should know that."

"I do," Caitlin agreed. "Do you often take a cigarette break?"

"No. Rarely," she said, as a disturbing thought occurred to her. *If I keep this baby, I won't be able to party with my friends. No smoking or alcohol for another seven months. And how am I going to support it? Mom can do it. She can pretend it's hers.*

"Any particular reason you needed one this time?" Caitlin asked. Hayley had said Olivia recognized her when she joined Jessica and had disappeared shortly afterward.

"No. I just wanted a smoke."

"Alright. How long were you outside?"

"Ten minutes."

"Then what did you do?"

"Went back inside."

"Why were you in that area?"

"I was checking supplies," she said.

"Why would you be looking behind a stack of empty cans?" Caitlin asked, adding a puzzled tone to her voice.

"Fine. I was taking a break and warming up after being outside. Satisfied?"

"Olivia, we can't solve this unless you answer truthfully," Ethan said.

"I am."

"Hayley said you were avoiding Corporal Smith. Why were you hiding?" he asked.

Her eyes blazing with anger, she pointed at Caitlin. "I didn't want to be her server because she embarrassed me."

"When?" Ethan asked.

"When she interviewed me."

"Corporal Smith is just doing her job," he said. "Please, answer our questions."

"I was trying to listen to her conversation with that blonde woman, so I squeezed in between two stacks of cans. Then everything fell on me," Olivia dabbed at her eyes.

"You're doing good, Olivia. Did you hear any other noises?" Ethan prompted.

"Like what?"

"I don't know exactly," he replied. He didn't want to lead her to an answer. "Maybe machinery. Or people talking. Or someone walking past. Anything."

"The only thing I can remember is that thing Rhys uses to move heavy stuff around. I heard it start up but I don't remember anything after that."

"Do you mean the forklift?" Ethan opened his phone and searched for an image, then turned it toward her. "Like this?"

"Yeah. That's it."

"And did you hear any other noises before the cans started to fall on you?"

Ethan's pulse quickened a little as Olivia turned her head, and looked down as if she was visualizing the accident.

"There was a loud scraping noise. Then the stack started to tilt and I screamed," she paused.

Caitlin caught Ethan's eye and nodded. She'd heard someone yell in surprise and pain.

"The cans showered over me, and something hard hit my head. I blacked out," Olivia said. Tears streamed down her face as she met Ethan's eyes and shakily asked, "Did someone really try to kill me? Do they hate me that much?"

"We don't know yet exactly what happened, but your information is very helpful and we appreciate your assistance," Caitlin said to Olivia, evading her plaintive questions. "Your mom is waiting to see you, so we'll stop now. If you remember any more details, here's my card with my phone number," she placed it on the bedside table and motioned for Ethan to do the same. Olivia obviously had a better rapport with him.

As Ethan and Caitlin stepped outside the cubicle, they nodded to Stephanie Ferguson. "We left our contact information with Olivia. If she remembers anything else about the incident, it would be helpful if she called us," Ethan said.

As they walked away, they could hear Olivia's mournful wail, "Mom! Someone tried to murder me!"

Caitlin locked eyes with Ethan and gave a tiny shrug. "She could be right. We just don't know for certain whether this was a targeted attack, or an accident and the person who caused it is too afraid to own up to their mistake."

"We should head back to the brewery. I'd like to ask Rhys, the head brewer, if there was any reason for someone to be using the forklift to move that stack of cans."

"Good plan."

Chapter 25

Cactus Brewing

Jessica called ahead to be sure that the brewery was open again, after Olivia's accident. Then she claimed a table in the taproom while Mike headed to the bar and placed their order. Carrying their beverages to the table, he set Jessica's down first, then his own.

"So, is this an actual date? Or are you nosing around?" he asked as he sat down.

"It's a date," she said. "With a little fact-finding mission thrown in."

Mike grinned at her. "But you didn't bring Sparky, your primary detective."

"Can't bring him inside the brewery, just the outside beer garden, which isn't open in December." She sipped her wine and smiled. "This is good. Thanks, love."

He nodded, indicating that he'd heard her. "What are you hoping to discover?"

"I want to ask Rhys if anyone was authorized to drive the forklift the day the stack tipped onto Olivia."

"I think that is something Caitlin or Ethan would have already asked."

"I'm curious, and they don't always share information with me."

"You're nosey. And the police aren't required to satisfy your curiosity."

Jessica turned her head as the front door opened. She lifted a hand and waved. "Speak of the devil, there's Caitlin and Ethan," she said to Mike.

"Hi, Jess. Hi, Mike. What are you doing here?" Caitlin asked as she came to a stop beside their table.

"We're on a lunch date. Care to join us?" she replied, then added, "Hey, Ethan. Good to see you."

"Hey yourself, Jess." He smiled at her. "Snooping, are you?"

"Who me? I wouldn't dare."

"I had nothing to do with the choice of restaurant for our so-called lunch date," Mike held up both hands, palms out. "Honest officer. It wasn't me."

Ethan extended his hand, and shook Mike's, "I believe you, bud. She's the slippery one."

"Seriously Jess, what's going on?" Caitlin asked.

"Sit down. You are too tall and you are giving me a sore neck." Jessica pushed a chair out with her foot. "Sit. Join us for lunch."

Ethan checked the time, "It's well past lunchtime, and I'm starving." He sat, then looked up at Caitlin.

"Fine, we'll have lunch," she turned to read the chalkboard. "What do you want? I'll put our order in."

"The pork tacos. And a club soda." Ethan leaned toward Jessica as Caitlin strode toward the bar, "You've annoyed her, again."

"It keeps our friendship interesting," Jessica whispered back.

"Why are you here, Jess?" Ethan asked.

She briefly considered evading his question, but decided to be truthful, "I was going to ask Rhys if anyone was authorized to use the forklift on the day that Olivia was hurt."

Ethan snorted. "That's why we're here, too." He didn't mention that they had been interviewing Olivia when he'd remembered his oversight.

"Great. Then we'll all be up to speed."

Caitlin reappeared with tall glasses of clear fizzy water. "Up to speed on what?"

"Details. Little details," Jessica replied.

Caitlin swung her green eyes to Ethan. "Care to elaborate, partner?"

Ethan pointed his chin at Jessica, "She's here to ask Rhys the same question that we came here to ask. Who was working that day that has a certificate to operate the forklift."

"I don't think a trained operator was driving the forklift," Jessica said.

"You already mentioned the tines should have been lowered when it was parked," Caitlin said. "But maybe when the stack tipped onto Olivia the driver panicked and ran."

"It's more than that," Jessica said. "The proper way to move those cans would be to lift individual pallets with the tines, and back away until clear of the stack, then lower the load for stability and to allow the driver to see. At that point, the driver would either set the load down in a clear area or drive it to the new location. A certified forklift operator wouldn't intentionally shove a whole stack of pallets and cans. It's ineffective and unsafe."

Mike nodded. "She's right. A trained person wouldn't have pushed the entire stack unless they intended to topple it."

"So, you think this was a deliberate attempt to hurt Olivia?" Ethan asked.

Jessica waggled her hand. "I don't know. It could have been inexperience on the part of an overzealous employee. Maybe someone who was trying to be helpful by restocking the line, or tidying up?"

"No one has come forward claiming responsibility," Caitlin said.

"If it was an accident, the person is probably too scared to admit it," Mike added.

"I agree," Caitlin said. "However, we have more information that leads us to think it was deliberate."

Jessica turned to Mike. "I told you. She's holding out on me!"

He swallowed a laugh as he caught the look on Caitlin's face.

"I'm not required to keep you apprised of an ongoing police investigation," Caitlin said, through tight lips.

"She's winding you up, partner," Ethan quietly interjected.

Jessica smiled at Caitlin and lightly punched her shoulder, "Ah, come on amiga. You know I'm teasing."

"Are you though?"

"Yes, I am. My apologies. It's too easy to get a rise out of you," Jessica said. "So, do you think it was deliberate?"

Caitlin stared at Jessica. "Seriously? You are still asking for confidential information?"

"Ya can't blame a girl for trying," she said as the waitress set their food on the table. "I'm starving. Let's eat."

Chapter 26

Cactus Brewing

The following morning, Rhys unlocked the rear door of the brewery and stepped inside. Post-Christmas staffing levels were still at a minimum to allow the administrative staff time off with their families, but some of their beers needed to be replenished.

Last night he added the lactobacillus and shut the burners off intentionally leaving the brew to sour overnight. This morning, he had to finish the process for their popular sour seasonal ale. It was time to fire the kettle up again for twenty minutes, to kill the lactobacillus, then let the brew rest before transferring the cool wort to the fermenter. He scanned the brewery, looking for Noah who was supposed to be helping out.

"Noah? Are you here?" His voice boomed across the empty brewery. "Noah?"

Tyler, the head chef, who was prepping food for their eleven o'clock opening, poked his head out of the kitchen. "What's up Rhys?"

"I'm looking for Noah. He's my helper today."

Tyler shook his head. "Haven't seen him yet."

"Okay thanks," Rhys said, frustration in his voice.

"Problems?"

"I'm going to have to talk to him. He's becoming unreliable."

"Do you need a hand with the brew?" Tyler asked.

"Thanks, I'll be fine. If Noah doesn't show up, I'll call Dylan in to cover for him," Rhys said.

"Gotcha." Then he retreated to his kitchen.

An hour later, the brew was ready to be moved to the fermenter, and Rhys started the transfer pump. It chugged for a few minutes then whirred, and slowed down. It wasn't common, but occasionally the intake would clog. A couple of minutes and it was good to go again.

Then it stopped again. He noticed the substance blocking the hose was odd. Slimy. Gelatinous. Not like anything he'd seen before. He opened the hatch of the kettle and looked inside, but couldn't see anything. He started the pump again, and it very quickly clogged. Perplexed, Rhys grabbed a wooden paddle and stirred the wort. A piece of fabric floated to the surface. Cursing at the stupidity of someone dropping garbage into the kettle and ruining the entire batch, he dragged the cloth to the side and reached to lift it out. The cloth was snagged on something heavy. Leaning in further, he saw what looked like a hand floating near the surface.

"What the hell?" He scrambled down the stairs and frantically pounded Sean's number on his cellphone. Yesterday, Noah had been wearing a similar shirt.

"Hey there," Sean answered.

"Sean, get down here now. We have a major problem."

"Now what's happened?"

"It's urgent. I'll show you when you get here."

Worried about Rhys's cryptic message, Sean phoned Piper and Reid, telling them they had another problem at the brewery. They all raced toward the brewery.

His voice shaking, Rhys explained to the small group how the pump clogged repeatedly, and about the odd substance in the pump filter, then told them about the shirt and said that he'd seen what looked like a hand floating in the kettle.

"Oh God, Rhys, are you sure?" Piper asked.

Rhys pointed at the kettle. "Have a look for yourself."

Sean exchanged worried looks with his partners, and Reid nodded toward the kettle. "We believe you Rhys, but Sean should take a quick look to confirm before we call emergency services."

Rhys handed Sean a flashlight. "You'll need this, and a strong stomach," he said grimly.

Sean reluctantly climbed the steps, opened the heavy metal hatch, and pointed the light inside. Gagging, he quickly shut the hatch, turning his pale face to the others. "Yep, it looks like a hand."

Piper phoned 9-1-1, explaining what Rhys had found, then disconnecting from emergency services, she sent a text to the phone number that Caitlin Smith had provided when Olivia was injured. *Please call me! It's an emergency. Piper Dawson, Cactus.*

Sean and Reid headed to the kitchen to let their staff know the taproom wouldn't be opening today, or perhaps for a few days. Amid groans from their staff about missed hours, they assured them that their wages would be covered until the problem was sorted out.

"I'll contact the waitstaff and let them know we are closed," Sean said to Piper and Reid.

"Okay. I'll contact Katie," Piper said as she tapped a message to their marketing manager, Katie Lewis. "She can get the word out about the temporary closure." *Please call me. We have a situation.*

Chapter 27

Cactus Brewing

Concentrating on not puking while vigorously chewing on a hard peppermint candy, Caitlin stood at the bottom of the stairway, leading to the kettle's hatchway. The FIS team, the Forensic Investigation Section of the RCMP, was occupied taking photos and gathering trace evidence.

The coroner, Amanda Christoper, stood by ready to extract the human remains from inside the stainless-steel vessel.

As soon as Amanda was given the all-clear by FIS, she directed Rhys and Sean to drain the remaining liquid into several clean containers which would be transported to the lab and strained for body tissue and evidence. When the grisly mess of cooked meat, clothing, and hair appeared, she slowly lowered herself into the tank.

Caitlin didn't know how Amanda coped with her job, but she knew she would need a couple of big glasses of something stronger than her usual glass of wine to dull the images and smells.

What the hell was going on here? Olivia had been badly injured, and now someone was dead. Very dead. Stewed overnight in a hot broth. The owners were overwhelmed.

She was fairly certain the body was Noah Atkins. According to the head brewer, Noah had been working yesterday, assisting with the latest batch. At some point Rhys noticed that Noah wasn't around, but assumed that he had left early. According to Rhys, Noah was known for being a slacker and not putting a lot of effort into his job.

Caitlin took a deep breath and dug her fingernails into her palms hoping the pain would distract her. Then she climbed the steps and poked her head over the rim of the hatch. "Can you tell me anything, Amanda?"

Her ghostly face surrounded by the white elasticized hood of her disposable body suit Amanda looked up. "You know I don't guess at the cause of death. I just pronounce and gather evidence. Dr. Liz will do the autopsy," she said, referring to the city morgue pathologist.

"Yeah, I know. But, I'm always hopeful for information that will help me get started immediately on solving this murder."

"Murder? You are that certain?"

"This opening is small. A person can't just fall into the kettle by accident, and who commits suicide by diving head first into a boiling vat of beer?"

"It could be an ale or a lager depending on the recipe. And, the liquid is called wort at this stage."

"Semantics. It is a boiling liquid. And we have a suspicious fatality."

"Until Dr. Liz confirms the cause of death, you're only guessing it's a murder."

"This isn't my first murder case," Caitlin said.

"Let's get this person to the morgue before you start chasing down suspects."

Caitlin clambered down the steps, standing to one side while Amanda and her assistants carefully scooped the bones, clothes, and overcooked flesh into plastic containers. Fighting the urge to gag, she swore off eating anything that resembled cooked pork. Or any meat cooked in beer. Or ale.

She approached the owners as they huddled together quietly discussing the tragedy. "I'm so sorry folks, but you'll have to remain closed until the pathologist, coroner, WorkSafe, Interior Health, and the RCMP, clear you for reopening."

Her face etched by worry, Piper nodded. "We understand. The safety of our staff and customers is paramount."

"We'll need statements from everyone who was working yesterday and today," Caitlin said. "And any customers that were here."

"We know which employees were here, that's the easy part," Reid Dawson said, "As for customers, some we can figure out through credit card receipts. Identifying anyone who paid cash?" He shook his head. "That might be impossible unless our staff remembers a particular person."

"I understand. We'll start by speaking to the employees that are here, then work on arranging interviews with anyone who worked yesterday but not today," Caitlin said, addressing the small group. "You understand that until we confirm with DNA, we don't know the unfortunate person's identity. Please don't tell anyone outside your immediate need-to-know staff what has happened here. We want the opportunity to inform his or her relatives first."

"Absolutely," Piper said, as Reid, Sean, and Rhys nodded in agreement.

Caitlin then turned to Rhys. "Can you tell me a bit about the brewing process?"

"Sure, what do you want to know?"

"Walk me through it. What do you and your helper do to make a batch of beer?" She held up her phone. "Would you mind if I recorded you? It's easier and more accurate than me scribbling in my notebook."

Rhys nodded. "That's fine. How technical do you want me to be?"

"I'm more interested in the timing of your activities, and when you noticed that Noah wasn't around," she said.

"Okay, starting at eight-thirty in the morning, we grind the grains and soak them in hot water, in the mash tun, to extract the sugars," he said.

"Mash tun?"

"That." He pointed at a stainless-steel vessel that was wider than it was tall. "Think of it as a huge pot of porridge."

"Okay. Then what?"

"Depending on the beer that we are making, mashing can take anywhere from an hour to several hours."

"And yesterday? How long did that process take?"

"Ninety minutes."

"What time would this process have finished?"

"Eleven."

"Eleven yesterday morning?"

"Yes."

"Was Noah still working with you at this point?"

"Yes, he was."

"What's next?"

"We drained the wort and transferred it to the kettle. This is called lautering. Then Noah started his cleanup tasks," Rhys said.

"Okay, keep going," Caitlin said, mentally dismissing the brewing lingo.

"We wait until the wort boils, then add the bittering hops."

Caitlin gave him a look. "I have no idea what that means, but who did it? You or Noah?"

"Me. I prefer to control how and when the hops are added. Any deviation can dramatically change the flavor of the brew." His face blanched. "Although in this case, it wouldn't have mattered."

"No, it wouldn't have," Caitlin said. "So what time are we at now?"

"Anywhere from noon to four-thirty in the afternoon," Rhys said.

"Could you be more precise?"

"Not really. I add the different hops at different times according to the recipe. I wasn't paying attention to Noah. He typically does the cleanup of the mash tun, the pumps, hoses, and other equipment while I pay attention to the brew."

"Was Noah still working during this time?"

Rhys chewed his bottom lip, and stared at the floor, "I honestly don't know where Noah was at this point. I was concentrating on adding the flavor hops thirty minutes before I shut off the kettle, and the aroma hops as soon as I turned off the heat."

Standing quietly as Rhys explained his brewing routine to Caitlin, Sean interjected, "Our production area is spread out and noisy. Noah could have been doing his regular tasks, and Rhys might not have seen or heard him."

Rhys nodded. "Exactly. With experienced workers, I don't track their every move. He could have been cleaning a tank, out of my line of sight."

Caitlin shut off the recording app, "Thanks Rhys, that helps me to better understand your routine."

"Anything else I can help with?" Rhys asked.

"Yes," she turned the app back on. "What time was it when you last opened the hatch on the kettle?"

"Four-thirty yesterday afternoon."

"Did you look inside then?"

"A brief glance. It isn't necessary, but it's a habit. One last look before I leave it for the night." He smiled briefly.

Reid spoke up. "Like putting a baby to bed at night."

"Yeah," Rhys agreed. "Like that."

"Do you always leave a brew overnight?" Caitlin asked.

"No, only when we are making our sour brews. Other recipes require us to transfer the cooling wort into a fermentation tank before leaving for the night."

She raised her eyebrows. "Two questions. What is a fermentation tank? And who would know that you were making a sour brew yesterday?"

Rhys turned and pointed at the larger tanks behind her, "Those are the fermentation tanks. That's where the sugars turn into alcohol. As for who knew we were making a sour..." he looked at the family. "Anyone can wander into the brewhouse and look at the schedule. It's posted on the wall."

"Okay, thank you for your help. That's all I can think of for now. Have I missed anything?" Caitlin asked.

"We're all too shocked to think at this point," Piper said.

Caitlin nodded. "I'm sure you are. In the meantime, here is my cell number if you think of anything else," she said, offering one of her RCMP contact cards to Rhys.

Chapter 28

Cactus Brewing

Caitlin turned and walked toward Ethan, who was deep in conversation with a thin-faced man wearing kitchen whites. Presumably the chef. Motioning to Ethan that she was going to interrupt the conversation, she asked, "Can I borrow you for a moment?"

"Sure." He turned to the man. "Please wait here. I'll be right back."

Caitlin motioned with her head to move out of earshot of the chef. "Is there anything that concerns you about him?"

"Not yet, but I haven't finished."

Caitlin mulled that over for a moment. "He's not a big guy. It would be a struggle for him to wrestle a body into the kettle."

"I know. But that could apply to most of the employees I've spoken to."

"Okay," she said. "What about Noah Atkins? Any luck locating him?"

Ethan shook his head. "Not me. Do you want me to ask Natalie if she has?"

"No, you carry on with the statements. I'll ask her."

Ethan nodded and returned to questioning the man.

Caitlin tapped Natalie's number in her phone, listening as it rang.

"Garcha."

"Hey Nat, where are you?"

"In the taproom, questioning the staff."

"Good. Have you tried to locate Noah Atkins?"

"No, was I supposed to?"

"No. I don't want to duplicate anything that you've already done," Caitlin said.

"Do you want me to ask the staff if anyone has seen him?"

Caitlin hesitated, weighing her options. Ask the staff and start them gossiping? Or ask his parents and cause them to worry? "Try to ask the question in a way that you are checking on the times and locations for more than one person. We need to limit social media gossip."

"Okay, will do," Natalie agreed.

Walking toward Piper, Caitlin asked, "Is there a private place where I can phone Noah's parents? I want to ask if he's been home since his shift yesterday."

Piper pointed at the open-plan upper mezzanine, "Conversations aren't private in this building. Perhaps out in the back alley? Or your car?"

"Good idea. I'll phone from my car. Do you have their number?"

"It should be in his employee file as his next of kin." Piper's face blanched. "I never in a million years thought I'd need it."

"Yeah. I know."

"Come with me, I'll get it for you."

Sitting in her police vehicle, Caitlin tapped her phone, calling the number for Noah's parents.

"Hello?"

"Hello. Is this Mrs. Atkins?"

"Yes. Who is this, please?"

"Corporal Caitlin Smith, of the Penticton RCMP. I'm sorry to disturb you, Mrs. Atkins. May I speak to Noah?" she replied, visualizing the worried expression that had probably settled on the other woman's face when she mentioned RCMP.

"What's wrong?" the woman asked with a sharp intake of breath.

"I'd like to speak to Noah, please."

"He's left for work," she said. "Is there a problem?"

"Are you sure he's not home?" Caitlin asked.

"Yes. When I called him for breakfast he didn't respond, so I checked his room. It's empty."

"Do you remember what time he came in last night?"

"We were asleep and didn't hear him," Mrs. Atkins said.

"Do you remember the last time that you spoke to Noah?"

"Yesterday, at breakfast? I think," Mrs. Atkins tentatively replied. "Is he in trouble? I know he smokes marijuana, but isn't it legal now?"

"That's not why I am calling, Mrs. Atkins. I just had a couple of questions for him about another matter. If you hear from him, please ask Noah to contact Corporal Smith at the Penticton detachment. If you have a pen handy, I will give you my cell phone number."

"Yes, of course. Go ahead," she said, writing as Caitlin recited the number. "I'll call him right now and give him your message."

"Thank you," Caitlin said, disconnecting the call. Noah's boiled phone was probably somewhere in the mess that Amanda and her team were currently scooping out of the kettle. She rolled her neck and rotated her shoulders, trying to loosen the tension in her knotted muscles.

She reluctantly climbed out of her vehicle and headed back inside. Dr. Liz would have to do a DNA test of course, but she was certain that Noah Atkins's remains were in the plastic bins, waiting to be transferred to the morgue.

"Did you find Noah?" Piper anxiously asked Caitlin.

"No. And his parents went to bed before he got home. Mrs. Atkins hasn't spoken to him since he left for work yesterday morning."

"Oh, dear God, what is going on?"

"Piper, I hate to ask this. Is there anything in the brewery that might have Noah's DNA on it?"

"Like what?"

"Any personal item from his locker could be helpful. A hairbrush or toothbrush would be the best, or something like a hat. One that you know is his. It might contain a strand of hair with the root intact."

"We don't have staff lockers for personal items," Piper said. "The workers wear our logoed caps, but they don't normally leave them here." She met Caitlin's eyes. "His cap could be in the kettle."

"Yes, it might. I'll visit Noah's parents next," Caitlin said as she tapped Noah's home address into Google Maps.

Chapter 29

Atkins' Home

Caitlin pulled her police vehicle to a stop in the driveway of a modest home in the Wiltsie neighborhood, only a few blocks away from where Sarah Wollman's family lived.

It was an area of well-kept homes with growing families, close to schools yet away from the bustle of the city. Entire blocks were engaged in a friendly competition of fanciful displays and holiday decorations. It appeared to be a safe place for children to mature into adulthood. And yet tragedy had struck twice. First Sarah. And now, quite possibly, Noah.

Glancing in her rearview mirror, she scowled at the deepening stress lines bracketing her dark green eyes, before stepping out of her car. As she closed the driver's door, a woman clutching a bulky red sweater around her thin body opened the front door and stood on the top step, watching Caitlin.

"Are you Corporal Smith?" she asked.

"Yes, ma'am. Are you Mrs. Atkins?"

"Yes. You'd better come in," she said, stepping back inside.

Caitlin wiped her boots on the entry mat and bent to remove them.

"It's okay, just leave them on. We'll sit in the kitchen."

"Thank you, ma'am," Caitlin said, then asked, "Is there anyone else at home Mrs. Atkins?"

"Please call me Laura," she said, avoiding Caitlin's eyes as if she could postpone whatever Caitlin wanted to tell her. "My husband, George is a long-distance truck driver. He is on the road and won't be home until late tonight."

"May I sit?" she asked, placing her hand on the back of the closest chair.

"Of course. Where are my manners? Would you like a cup of tea?"

Caitlin smiled gently. "Yes, thank you." A cup of strong, hot tea might do them both some good.

Turning her back, Laura filled the kettle. "Is Noah in trouble?" she asked.

"No ma'am. There has been an accident at the brewery, and we are trying to locate Noah. Have you heard anything from him?"

"No. I've left several messages for him, but he hasn't called back." She plugged in the kettle and turned to Caitlin, "What kind of accident?"

Caitlin stood and gently took Laura's arm, guiding her to the table. "Please, sit, Laura."

"What kind of accident?" She repeated, slowly sinking onto the chair.

"Someone has died, but we don't know who."

"What do you mean? How could you not know who died?" her voice wobbled.

"Mrs. Atkins, Laura, please don't assume the worst. We are trying to eliminate anyone who we can't account for. I'm hoping you have a hairbrush or toothbrush of Noah's so that we can do a DNA comparison."

"That will take weeks! I have to find my son, right now," she said searching for her phone.

"There is a quicker method available now, but we need something to compare to," Caitlin reassured her.

"I need to know what's going on. Where is my son?"

"We are trying our best to find him, Laura. In the meantime, we want to eliminate him from our investigation. Would you be able to find something personal of Noah's?"

Laura rose unsteadily from her chair, placing one hand on the tabletop to steady herself. She slowly put one foot in front of the other, walking the length of the hallway. Caitlin stood, watching carefully for any signs that the woman might faint or stumble. She should have someone at home with her, for support.

Returning a few minutes later, Laura said, "This is Noah's," and handed Caitlin a black-handled brush, entangled with dark hairs.

Caitlin slipped it into an evidence bag, then shoved it deep into the side pocket of her parka. "May I call someone for you, Laura? Someone to be with you until your husband returns? Perhaps a neighbor?"

"I'll be fine."

"It would be better to have someone with you, to share the worry until Noah returns your messages," Caitlin said. "Let me call someone for you."

"I'll do it," Laura picked up her phone and tapped a number. "Susie, it's me. Can you come over?" she asked softly.

Caitlin heard a female voice reply, "Sure. When?"

"Right away?" Laura said, her voice breaking into sobs. Still clutching the phone, her hand dropped to her lap.

"Laura, what's going on?" the voice asked. "Laura? Laura!"

Reaching out, Caitlin gently lifted the phone from her hand. "This is Corporal Smith from the Penticton RCMP. Laura could use a friendly shoulder to lean on."

"What's happened?" Susie demanded.

"We are having difficulty locating Noah," Caitlin replied.

"Oh God, okay. I'll be there in five minutes."

Disconnecting, Caitlin placed Laura's phone on the table, then moved to the counter. "Now, where do you keep your tea?" As her English granny was fond of saying, a strong brew of hot sugary tea was the best remedy for all the woes of the world. *If only that was true.*

While she waited for the tea to steep, Caitlin tapped a message to Ethan.

Got his hairbrush. Waiting for a friend to arrive for support. Need a quick turnaround on DNA.

A few seconds later, Ethan's thumbs-up pinged on her phone.

Chapter 30

Cactus Brewing

In the alley behind the brewery, Jessica observed Sparky as he vacuumed up a variety of scents. The DNA test had confirmed that it was Noah's body inside the kettle, and Caitlin was searching for anything that could help solve this case.

What mysterious mix of odors was he smelling? Other dogs certainly. Birds. Deer. A variety of people walking through the area. Maybe a raccoon or a stray cat had wandered past. She watched as he sniffed around the garbage bins, but wasn't worried that he'd find something disgusting and eat it. Unlike some of her previous dogs, Sparky wasn't a food hound, and even if he found something edible, she doubted that he'd eat it... unless it was presented to him on a clean plate.

She slowly followed him as he wandered through the back entrance into the brewery, stopping numerous times in the area where Olivia had been injured, then continuing to the kettle where Noah had died, gruesomely.

Sparky put one front paw on the metal gridwork, then removed it and turned to look up at Jessica. He clearly wanted to climb the stairs, but didn't like the sensation of the perforated metal against his paws.

"Do you mind if I carry Sparky up the stairs?" she asked, Caitlin. "I think he wants to investigate, but he won't walk on the metal grid."

Caitlin stood a few feet away, her head tilted to one side, studying the equipment. "Go ahead. Can you lift him, or do you need a hand?"

"He's solid, but I can lift him," Jessica said and bent down. "Hugs, Sparky." He boosted himself into her outstretched arms, and she hoisted him up until his front paws were draped over her left shoulder. Aware that she was probably breaking at least six or seven health and safety codes, she climbed the short stairway with a one-handed death grip on the railing.

Setting Sparky down at the top, she waited to see what he would do.

"What's he doing?" Caitlin asked.

"He's smelling the step and the side of the kettle. It's a good thing it isn't on or he'd scorch his nose." Jessica replied over her shoulder, then spoke quietly to her dog, "What's caught your interest, pooch?"

"Pardon? I didn't hear you," Caitlin said.

"I was talking to Sparky," Jessica replied, casting a quick look in Caitlin's direction. Caitlin was still standing with her head tilted to one side like a baffled dog. "What are you puzzling over?"

"The physics of shoving a person through the hatchway and into the kettle. It would take strength. And surprise."

Jessica studied the hatch and was relieved that it was securely closed, preventing her from peering inside the death chamber. "The entrance isn't very big. The assailant would have to restrain a young, reasonably fit person, and keep him from shouting for help while he stuffed him into the kettle, or hit him over the head hard enough to knock him unconscious and then stuff him inside."

"Easier with two people," Caitlin said.

"You could be right, except there isn't much space in this area for a wrestling match between two assailants and their victim."

"Stop shooting down my theories," Caitlin objected, mildly. "Has Sparky found anything?"

"Well, he's scoured the area where Olivia was injured and eventually led me here," she said motioning to where she stood on the top step. "I think he might have matched the scent, or scents, of the culprits for both incidents."

Surprised, Caitlin looked up at Sparky, "Can he do that? Is he that smart?"

"He's smart, alright," Jessica said. "I just wish he could talk. It would make life simpler."

Caitlin snorted a laugh. "Simpler? He'd be ordering you around with actual words instead of his impressive repertoire of snorts, sneezes, and eyebrow twitches."

"Yeah, you're right," Jessica said. "Are you done here pooch?"

He looked up at her and briefly wagged his tail.

"Okay, I'll carry you down. Carefully." She bent over and scooped him into her arms, then slung him over her left shoulder again, leaving her stronger right hand free to grip the handrail as she backed down.

"Are you okay?" Caitlin asked.

"Yep, I'll back down."

"Wait a sec," Caitlin said as she stepped up to Jessica's level, and peered around her shoulder. "I see what you mean about not enough room for three people. It would be too tight."

"Yep, two assailants wouldn't fit."

"Could two people carry an unconscious person up these steps?" Caitlin wondered aloud.

"I don't think so. An unconscious person is difficult to carry, feels heavier than if they are conscious, and tends to flop about."

"How do you know that?"

"My brother Jake. When he was a teenager and doing something stupid, he smacked his head and knocked himself out. Matt and I carried him inside the house. It was difficult."

"Hmm. Okay, let's get you and Sparky off this thing," Caitlin said and placed her palm firmly in the middle of Jessica's back. "I've seen firefighters do this when someone is backing down a ladder. It helps with their stability."

"It's only four steps. I should be fine."

"One tall step, and three regular ones. For once, just do as I ask," Caitlin said.

"Fine. What do you want me to do?"

"Just step back, when I say 'step,' use your toe to feel for the tread and I'll match your movements."

When Jessica had both feet back on the floor, she turned, and set Sparky down. "It might be time for you to go on a diet, pooch."

"He is a solid little dude," Caitlin said, examining the kettle. "I can't figure out how someone could overpower Noah, then disappear without being noticed."

"Someone who works here?"

"We've interviewed all of the owners and employees. Everyone has an alibi of sorts. Some have alibis from other employees who were on shift during the timeframe. Others have family members who can confirm their whereabouts," Caitlin said.

"But if two people were in on it, and are each other's alibis, how can you be sure who is telling the truth and who isn't?"

"We just proved that it would be a tight fit for two assailants."

"Granted. But maybe one was the lookout. And the other was the attacker," Jessica replied.

"Possible. We are cross-checking everyone's stories for motive, means, and opportunity."

"What about the incident involving Olivia? And Sarah's death? Are they connected to this?"

Caitlin leaned against a counter. "We've been trying to find a connection, but so far nothing, other than graduating from the same high school a couple of years ago, and then working here. Sarah only briefly. Olivia, and Noah a little longer."

"What about the guy at the condo? Payback for the kids using his drugs?"

"If Olivia, Hayley, and Noah are to be believed, they only helped themselves to a handful of pills," Caitlin explained. "Murder as payback seems a stretch, however, we are investigating that angle too. He's disappeared, but we were able to confirm the guy's real name. He already has one outstanding Canada-wide arrest warrant for failure to appear in court on another matter, and now we want him for questioning in relation to Sarah's death."

"Who is he?"

Raising one eyebrow, Caitlin looked at her. "Do you remember any of our previous conversations? Me cop. You civilian."

Chuckling, Jessica clipped Sparky's leash to his harness. "For a moment there, I thought we were bonding so well. Kinda like Cagney and Lacey."

"We weren't even born when that show was popular."

"I've watched reruns."

"That's weird," Caitlin said, then asked, "The usual fee for Sparky's services?"

"Yep. Dried liver treats and he's a happy boy." Jessica eyed the kettle, distastefully, and shuddered.

"What's with the face?"

"I won't ever be able to drink their beer again unless they replace the kettle, the pump, and whatever else touched that batch," Jessica said. "Just the thought of what happened here turns my stomach, and I don't think I'm the only one."

"I hadn't thought about that," Caitlin said. "The loss of business. An extended shutdown for equipment replacement, particularly the kettle which, I think, is a custom-made item taking several weeks to build. Then a thorough sanitizing."

"Have you considered that the attacks might have been aimed at the four co-owners, not the employees? As an attempt to put them out of business?"

Caitlin said dropped her chin and mumbled. "Fricking hell. Other breweries. Suppliers. Bar owners. That is a gigantic list of new suspects."

"Yep."

Tapping a well-used number on her phone, Caitlin waited for it to be answered. "Hi, boss. I'm going to need more help. Our two suspicious deaths and the suspicious incident might be interconnected."

The deep, rough voice of Sergeant Williams asked, "How soon can you get here?"

"I'll be there in five."

"Meet me in the incident room."

"Yes, sir." Disconnecting, Caitlin looked at Jessica. "I've got to brief the boss on your newest theory."

Jessica pointed at Caitlin, then herself, "It's our theory, but if you are passing out *atta boys* you can include a pat for Sparky."

"Not until we arrest the bad guys."

"Give Sergeant Williams a belated Christmas hug from me," Jessica said, her eyes crinkling in laughter.

"He'll be thrilled."

Chapter 31

Penticton RCMP station

In the incident room, Sergeant Williams stood in front of the whiteboard, as if being closer to the scribbled notes and photos would yield a solution to the puzzle. Three major incidents. They had days, if not hours, to solve these cases before SCU would insist on taking them over. In the end, all that mattered was the perpetrators were brought to justice, but he wanted his team to find the solution, and to get the accolades. And perhaps a promotion for Caitlin, although he'd hate to lose her.

As the NCO i/c, the Non-Commissioned Officer in charge of the Penticton General Investigative Section he was her boss and her mentor. The RCMP Serious Crime Unit, based out of the larger city of Kelowna was pushing to take over these cases. He was able to hold them off, temporarily, because the two deaths were still classified as suspicious accidents, not deliberate acts of malice.

The moment that SCU decided that Sarah Wollman and Noah Atkins had been murdered, Caitlin would be reassigned to just the Olivia Caponera accident. Even that might be taken from her, if, as Caitlin suspected, it was linked to the two deaths. She was his top investigator, and he wanted her to handle the cases to the finish line. He would fight for Caitlin and her team through as many bosses as it took.

Encumbered at birth with a double name, William Williams, he had become a resilient scrapper to keep from being bullied as a youngster. Even some adults thought he was being impertinent when they asked his name and he replied, William Williams. His worn face creased in a wry grin. Since he had joined the police force, many years ago, no one had taunted him about his name, at least not to his face. Perhaps the gun on his hip, and the badge in his pocket had something to do with that.

"Hey boss," Caitlin said, breezing through the door as she shed her jacket and cap. "Thanks for meeting with me so quickly."

"What have you discovered?"

"I have a new theory that I want to run past you."

"Fire away," he said, resting his ample butt cheek against the closest desk.

"I think there is a possibility that my three cases are linked. That it's a vendetta against the Dawson family."

"Evidence?" Williams asked, as his thick grey eyebrows scrunched closer together.

"Not solid evidence. But, all three of the young people worked for Cactus Brewery. Two are dead. One was badly injured, and perhaps was meant to be dead as well."

"Coincidence. And you know cops don't like that word."

"It was Jessica Sanderson who put the idea in my head, but let me explain, Sarge."

Williams sighed. "Jessica. I should have known."

"I know, she can be annoying. And she can be annoyingly right, too."

He twitched one shoulder acknowledging her observation. "Why would anyone have a vendetta against a well-liked local family, who supports numerous community fundraisers and events? Who could possibly dislike them?" Williams asked.

"As Jessica pointed out, the thought of someone dying in the kettle was enough to put her off purchasing their product for quite some time, and it could take several weeks before the brewery can re-open. The kettle and any other equipment, like the hoses and pumps, that came in contact with Noah Atkins's body will have to be replaced. The kettle is almost certainly a custom order. The delay and expense will be massive. And who benefits? The other local craft breweries, or maybe a competing bar owner."

"Before you open that can of worms, what about their staff? Have you cleared everyone?"

"We interviewed everyone and they all have solid alibis, except Dylan Hughes."

"Who is Dylan Hughes?"

"An assistant brewer who was working in the brewhouse when Olivia Caponera was attacked. We couldn't find him right away. He showed up a few minutes later with the explanation that he had been working in the cooler, and it was quite soundproof.

Also, he was wearing his EarPods and according to him, listening to music."

"What is your gut reaction to him?"

"I think he is in the clear. The only connection between Olivia and Dylan is they both work at the brewery, and he wasn't working the day that Noah died."

"Okay. What do you need from me?"

"We'll need a larger team to question the competitors and their employees."

"I'm trying to prevent SCU from scooping your cases. More staff will draw more attention."

"I know boss, and I appreciate that, but the four of us, Ethan, Evan, Natalie, and me are working flat out. We won't be able to efficiently handle the increase in information without some assistance. We can handle the interviewing, if you can find us a couple of people to organize the incoming data, manage the whiteboard, and update the murder book."

"What if this is the work of an unhappy customer?"

"Kill someone because you didn't like your meal? It's possible, but it seems less likely," Caitlin said, studying Williams. She worried about his health. His grey pallor, rounded shoulders, and chubby dad-body, made him look older than his fifty-two years. Or was he fifty-three now? The deep crevices on either side of his wide mouth added years to his face. His happy home life struggled to offset the many stressful nights worrying about the safety of himself or fellow officers, and a substandard diet of junk food hastily eaten while working.

"Alright. I'll find you a few more helpers. But, if the Superintendent gets pressure from SCU, we won't be able to hold them off for more than a day or two."

"Yes, sir, I know."

"What's next?"

"I think my best plan of action is to start with the other brewery owners. Including Cactus there are about eleven craft breweries in our immediate area," she said, jotting a list of names on the whiteboard.

"What about the one in Oliver?"

"Good point. That's in our jurisdiction too," Caitlin said and added it to the list.

Williams gave her a shrewd look. "I assume you won't be venturing north into Kelowna with your brewery inquiries, just yet?"

"No, I don't want SCU to figure out what I'm up to," she said. "We'll talk to the local owners first, then the employees. If nothing pops up, and we haven't been shut down by SCU, we'll move on to the proprietors of the large pubs, bars, and restaurants."

"Alright. Get your team on it. We'll keep things moving here."

"Thanks, boss. I appreciate your confidence in us," she picked up her jacket, and shoved one arm inside.

"Wait a second," Williams said. "How are you doing?"

"I'm fine boss."

"Cut the crap. A person cooked in a kettle is not an everyday occurrence. So, I'll ask again. How are you doing?" Williams asked.

She let her jacket slide off her arm, and placed both hands on the back of a chair, preventing them from trembling. "It is a horrific way for anyone to die, and worse because he was only twenty. He had his whole life ahead of him. It's a God-awful waste."

"I agree. Are you getting any sleep?"

"Enough," she replied, thinking about the snippets of dark dreams and realizing in the morning, that her body and the bottom sheet, were the only things still on the bed. Everything else was on the floor.

"And Ethan? How's he doing?"

"He's coping, but I think it has hit him harder. They have a young son, Rowan, and Ethan worries about the what-ifs. What if something like this happened to their son?"

Williams nodded. "I still worry about my two grown kids, hoping they live to a very old age and become a nuisance to their children."

"Like you are going to be for your kids?"

"Going to be? I already am," Williams said.

Caitlin smiled at that.

"Take advantage of the paid counseling. Both of you," he said.

"Will do, boss," she said. At the door, she stopped and turned around, "I almost forgot. Jessica wanted me to give you a belated Christmas hug," she said holding her arms out wide, inviting him in for an embrace.

"Bah humbug!" he said, shooing her away.

Laughing at his predictable reaction, Caitlin waved goodbye. Williams pretended not to like Jessica, while Jessica dramatically overplayed her affection for him, but underneath the bantering, there was a mutual respect between the two.

Chapter 32

Caponera-Ferguson home

Olivia languished in her comfortable bed, happy to have her mother fussing over her, like she did before Kent arrived. Since their marriage, Kent's needs dominated their lives and monopolized her mother's love, leaving Olivia feeling angry and alone.

Stephanie placed her hand on Olivia's. "How are you feeling sweetie? Can I get you anything?"

"I'm tired and scared, Mom."

"Scared?"

Theatrically squeezing a couple of tears from her eyes, "I'm too afraid to go back to work until my attacker is in jail," she said, happy to have an excuse for not returning to work.

"I understand dear, and I've spoken to your boss. She will hold your job for you until you feel better."

"Didn't the police close the brewery after the attempt on my life?" Olivia said.

"They did, but only for a few hours," Stephanie said.

"Hmph! Well, it could be a while before I am strong enough to return to work," she said, sighing listlessly.

"There's no rush," Stephanie said. "I have a surprise for you. Hayley is downstairs. She has come for a visit."

"Hayley. Why?"

"She's your closest friend, and she wants to make sure you are okay."

"Fine. But, just for a few minutes."

Stephanie gave her daughter a puzzled look. "Alright, I won't let her stay too long," she said.

A couple of minutes later Hayley rushed into her bedroom, "Livy! Oh, my God. I'm so glad you weren't killed!"

"It was very close," Olivia replied. "I can still hear that awful noise and feel the terror of being buried alive." No one, not her mother or her friends, needed to know that she only remembered screaming once, and then something hit her on the head. The next thing she knew, she was on a stretcher and being rushed to the hospital. As far as she knew, no one had witnessed the accident, so she could tell her story any way she wanted.

Hayley said, "I heard a high-pitched scream, and then it stopped suddenly. I didn't know where you were and I was terrified." Her eyes sparkled with excitement. "Tell me everything!"

Olivia gingerly pointed at her head and carefully raised her broken arm an inch or two. "These are my visible injuries, but I am still terrified."

"Oh Livy, I can't imagine. What was it like?"

"I want to do a podcast then you and my followers will understand what I went through, to experience my fear," Olivia said with a shiver. "When I reenact the event, it could help the police find the criminal who tried to murder me."

"Are you sure it wasn't an accident?" Hayley asked.

"It was an attempt on my life!"

"Sorry, I was just asking," Hayley replied. "Do you know how to do a podcast?"

"Well, no, but Noah's a computer geek. He can do the setup. I'll be the on-air personality." She arranged her face in what she believed was a heart-rending pose and snapped a selfie.

"Why would you want to involve Noah? He's a boring pain in the butt."

"He's useful and everyone wants to be my friend, even geeks like Noah."

Humbled, Hayley toyed with her phone. "Is that what you think about me, Livy? That I'm just a hanger-on?"

"You? No, of course not," she said, brushing aside Hayley's question. "We're besties! Scoot in beside me, and we can take selfies with my injuries."

Olivia snapped several poses. She tried a variety of somber, sad, and unhappy expressions, while Hayley strived for concerned and caring.

Previewing the photos, Olivia decided on one that in her opinion showed her as a tough survivor. She posted it to her social media accounts, with a teaser saying full details to follow in an upcoming podcast.

"Have you heard from Lucas?" Hayley asked.

"No. Why?" Olivia searched her friend's face. *Does she know I'm pregnant?*

"Just curious. I like that other guy, Connor. I was wondering if he's still around."

Olivia exhaled relieved. "Lucas said he didn't want to see us again. He was really angry when we wanted to call the ambulance for Sarah. I think he deals and he was worried about the cops finding out."

"I get that. But, Connor, he was nice. I'd like to see him again."

"He's just a guy, Hayley. There are lots of other guys."

"Not like Connor."

"You had sex with him. Once. You know nothing about him," Olivia said. "Stay away from the condo, Hayley. Lucas is scary when he's angry. Maybe in a couple of months he'll relax and let us come back, but not right now."

"Yeah, okay," Hayley said. "Livy, did Sarah take the drugs herself? Or did Lucas spike that Christmas drink he made for us?"

"Why would you ask that?" Olivia hedged.

"The cops asked if I had seen Sarah take the drugs. I said no, and it's true. I didn't see her actually pop any pills. I've been wondering if Lucas added something to her drink. He had his back turned, but I noticed his hands were hovering over one glass in particular. Then instead of letting us choose a glass, he handed them out, like he wanted to control who got which one."

"He was just being a good host," Olivia said, defensively. The memory of Lucas stirring the liquid in one of the glasses with a spoon had been buried until now. Her right hand made slow, soothing circles on her abdomen as the images played in her mind.

Did he spike Sarah's drink? Had she subtly encouraged him because Sarah was whining about going home in an hour?

Watching Olivia rub the area below her belly button for the third time, Hayley asked. "Does your stomach hurt too?"

Olivia jerked her hand away. "No. Why did you ask that?"

"You keep touching and rubbing your belly like it hurts."

"What do you mean, my belly? Don't you dare call me fat," she retorted.

"Livy, I didn't mean that you were fat. I just said you were rubbing that area as if you were in pain."

"There is nothing wrong with my stomach. It's just a habit," she snapped. "I'm tired. Just go."

"Please don't be mad at me. I didn't mean to upset you."

"I'm tired and I have a horrible headache. I think I have a concussion. Please just go."

"Do you want me to ask Noah about helping with your podcast?"

Canned by Lynda L. Lock

"I'll text him myself," Olivia replied curtly.

"Okay. Text me if you need anything, or just want to hang out," Hayley said.

"I need my rest. I'll let you know when I feel up for another visit."

Hayley slowly walked backward toward the door. "Please don't be mad at me."

"It's fine."

Waiting until Hayley shut the bedroom door, Olivia scoured the internet for information on pregnancies. She had been thinking about her situation while talking with Hayley and had unconsciously been rubbing her belly.

She wasn't completely certain who the father was. It was probably Lucas because he was the one that she had slept with most often. He was fun for sex, but after seeing his violent reaction when Sarah needed help, she didn't want to be tied to him for the rest of her life just because of a baby. There were also a couple of other one-night stands, guys that she didn't know all that well, and didn't want to know.

It infuriated her that she was using a contraceptive, and still became pregnant. "I should sue the fricking pharmaceutical company," she groused.

How was she going to break the news to her mother, and convince her not to share her embarrassing situation with Kent?

Have the baby? Have an abortion? Give it up for adoption? That decision could wait for a bit, but how long? How soon would she start to show? I'll

197

think about that tomorrow. In the meantime, I have a podcast to organize.

She sent a text to Noah.

Hi. Have an amazing idea. Need your help.

She waited, watching the line of text. Waiting for the notification that the message had been received and read.

"Come on, Noah. Check your phone."

Nothing.

She sent a second message.

Nothing.

"Loser. I'll find someone else to help me," she taunted the silent phone.

Tossing back the covers on her bed, she stiffly set her feet on the floor and eased her way over to her cupboard, where she began to rummage through her clothes.

While she searched for the perfect outfit to accentuate her best features, she rattled off a monologue of ideas to herself. "I can turn my tragedy into an ongoing podcast with daily updates on the investigation. It will need a punchy title, something that will intrigue people. When I make money from my subscribers I'll quit my lame waitressing job."

Standing in front of her full-length mirror she studied her face, turning it from side to side. "For my first episode, I should look more injured. More battered and bruised. A bit of makeup will help create the illusion of two black eyes, and increase the sympathy factor."

She gingerly pulled up the sleeves of her sleeping shirt, checking the grab marks that Lucas had left around her upper arms on Christmas morning. "It's a good thing Mom hasn't noticed these. It would be pretty hard to explain how I got them." She pulled her sleeves down, staring at her image.

Hayley might be infatuated with Connor, but she now had a clearer image of what Lucas was really like. Dangerous and self-centered.

Chapter 33

Penticton RCMP station

Caitlin's desk phone buzzed with an internal call. "This is Smith," she said.

"Caitlin, there are people here to see you," the civilian report taker said.

"Who?"

"Mr. and Mrs. Wollman."

Surprised, Caitlin wondered what had brought them to the station. The logical reason was they were looking for an update on their daughter's case.

"Caitlin?"

"I'll be right there," she said and disconnected.

She had a second surprise when she saw Barry Kramer, a lawyer she recognized, standing beside Ed Wollman. Nodding to the civilian, she indicated that the Wollmans and their lawyer could be buzzed into the secure area.

"Ed, Irene. How are you doing?" Caitlin asked.

Ed silently looked at the floor.

"About how you would expect," Irene answered through tight lips.

"Yes, of course. Come with me, please," she said leading them into a small conference room. "What can I do for you?" Caitlin asked.

Kramer held up his hand to stop the Wollmans from responding, and said, "Mr. and Mrs. Wollman are volunteering to clarify what happened at the brewery on the afternoon of December 27th."

"Do you mean at Cactus Brewing, where Noah Atkins died?"

"Yes," Kramer responded.

"I'll have to move this conversation into an interview room and include another officer. Can you give me five minutes to arrange that?" she said.

Kramer nodded unhappily.

Once they were settled in an interview room, Caitlin recited the required legal caution, then began her questioning.

"Tell me in your own words what happened on the afternoon of December 27th," Caitlin said, to both Irene and Ed Wollman.

Normally a formal interview would be conducted with only one suspect, but the Wollmans asked to speak to her together. She'd decided to attempt a joint interview, hoping the interplay between husband and wife would provide her with more answers.

Ethan Jones sat quietly by her side. He'd expressed his doubts about the idea but agreed that it was worth a try. They could always halt the interview, and separate the Wollmans.

"We went to the brewery just to talk to Noah. To explain how devastated we were. He wouldn't listen," Ed Wollman said, his eyes begging for understanding.

Irene's face flushed as her hands gestured angrily. "At the party on Christmas Eve, Noah just sat there and let our beautiful girl die while he was sitting less than ten feet away."

"Noah said he fell asleep," Caitlin replied, recalling the devastated reaction of Noah's parents when she informed them of their son's death. "He didn't know that Sarah had stopped breathing."

"He should have been looking out for her. Who goes to a party and lets a friend die?" Irene Wollman snapped at Caitlin.

"Parties are very different from when I was her age," Caitlin said. "Now the kids travel as a group, not as couples. No one is designated as a minder, to watch out for the others. Plus, there are many more dangerous drugs available now."

"Are you making excuses for them letting her die like that?" Irene asked.

"Not at all, but the prosecutor believes that Noah wasn't criminally at fault," Caitlin replied.

"Then Olivia, and that other girl Hayley are to blame for forcing her to drive them to the party," Irene answered again, jumping in before her husband could respond. "Teenage girls can be brutal, and Sarah just wanted them to like her."

Caitlin remained silent.

"She's guilty of killing my girl," Irene sobbed into her hands.

"The person who gave Sarah the spiked drink is the one you should be angry with," Caitlin replied.

Ed touched Irene's arm, signaling her to let him speak, "You'll never find him. He's some drug-dealing low-life who has moved on to another town already," he said.

"His description and a current photo have been circulated to every police service across Canada and the border services agency. He can't leave by plane or vehicle or ship without having his passport scanned," Caitlin said. "We haven't given up."

"He can sneak across into the USA at any number of unmanned locations. He's probably already supplying drugs to other young people," Irene replied bitterly.

"We are getting off-track. Can you walk us through what happened at the brewery?" Caitlin asked.

The Wollmans exchanged a look, then he met Caitlin's scrutinizing gaze. "It was an accident."

Carefully keeping the disbelief out of her voice, Caitlin said, "What was an accident?"

"We were upset. We went to the brewery to talk to Noah. To find out who gave our lovely daughter the drugs. He claimed he didn't know," Ed replied.

"He kept saying it wasn't his fault," Irene said, swiping at her face with a tissue, "He denied everything."

"And then what happened?"

Barry Kramer spoke forcefully, "Ed, Irene. We've discussed this. Do not answer that question."

"We aren't bad people. We want to clear the air. As I said it was an accident," Ed repeated.

"Can you explain that?" Caitlin prompted again.

"He was standing at the top of that metal staircase, nervously fiddling with the lock on the hatch. He wouldn't meet my eye. Just kept flicking at the lock. Open. Closed. Open. Closed. I just wanted him to acknowledge that he was to blame for my daughter's death."

"He just wouldn't accept responsibility," Irene wailed. "He kept denying that it was his fault."

Caitlin waited; her chest tight with anticipation.

"I was angry, and grieving. I hit him." Ed said.

"What with?" They had searched the brewery and couldn't find anything that had been used as a weapon.

"My fist." Ed lifted his hands from his lap and set them on the table, displaying scabbed cuts on three knuckles of his right hand.

"And then what happened?" Caitlin's face registered surprise.

"Noah collapsed. I checked for a pulse but couldn't find one."

"Mr. Wollman, did you put Noah in the kettle?" Caitlin asked.

"Yes, I panicked and wanted to hide his body. I figured it would confuse the timing if they couldn't find him right away, and it would give me time to create an alibi."

"And what were you doing at this time, Mrs. Wollman?"

"I was hysterical. I couldn't think straight," she said. Her eyes were aimed at her own hands that repeatedly twisted a damp tissue.

"How did you manage to get Noah into the kettle?" Caitlin asked. This was the biggest question that she couldn't answer.

"I've worked as a bricklayer and a stone mason for thirty years. I may not have the build of a weightlifter, but I am strong. I lifted him by myself. Irene had nothing to do with this."

"She was with you. She saw you punch Noah. And she witnessed you putting him into the kettle."

"She had nothing to do with it. I lost my temper and punched him. It's my fault. I killed him by accident."

"Mr. Wollman, Noah's lungs had liquid in them."

"What does that mean?"

"He was alive when you dumped him inside the kettle. He drowned in the boiling liquid," Caitlin said.

"No! That can't be right," his face drained of color. "You saw me, Irene, I checked for a pulse. He was dead."

"Yes, Ed checked. He was dead!" Irene shouted.

"The pathologist's preliminary report says he wasn't."

"It was an accident. An accident!" Irene yelled.

"That's enough," Kramer said. "I'm stopping this interview."

Caitlin shot her partner a look, and they stood in unison, "Mr. Wollman, please stand," she said. Ethan removed the handcuffs from his belt and stood behind Wollman.

"I am arresting you on one count of homicide in the death of Noah Atkins," Ethan said and continued reciting the required statement of an arresting officer.

"It was an accident," Irene Wollman continued to mumble over and over, "an accident."

Kramer put his arm around Irene, letting her lean into him as her husband was led out of the room toward the holding cells.

"Mrs. Wollman, we have more questions for you, but you are free to leave and take care of your son," Caitlin said. "Please be back here at the station tomorrow morning at nine."

"Why?" Irene pulled away from Kramer and clasped her trembling hands together.

"You just implicated yourself in the coverup of Noah Atkins's murder. Be here at nine tomorrow morning."

Noticing Irene's increased distress, Kramer asked, "Is that absolutely necessary, Corporal Smith?"

"Yes, it is, Mr. Kramer. We want to question Mrs. Wollman separately from her husband about Noah's death, and also about a previous serious incident involving another person who was at the party with Sarah," she replied. *Judging by his confused expression, Kramer doesn't have a clue what I am talking about. Interesting that his clients had neglected to mention the other incident.*

Chapter 34

Penticton RCMP station

After Ed Wollman was tucked away in a cell, and Irene and their lawyer were escorted out the door, Caitlin perched on Ethan's desk with one foot resting on the floor, the other dangling from the edge, "What does your gut tell you?"

"I think both of them put Noah in the kettle. An unconscious or dead body is hard to handle on your own. My money is on Ed lifting the heavier head end, and Irene the feet," Ethan said.

"I agree. What I can't figure out is how they did it without being seen, or heard, by Rhys, the head brewer."

"We didn't ask Ed what time their confrontation happened. Maybe Rhys had left for the day."

"True. We'll continue Ed's interview tomorrow, separate from Irene. See if we can pin him down on details and then cross-check with Irene's answers. Their argument with Noah would have been loud enough for someone else to hear them, wouldn't you think?"

Ethan nodded. "You would think so. Maybe they had a lookout, watching for other staff."

"Involving a third person?" Caitlin made a face. "That's getting complicated."

"They have a teenage son. When Natalie did the next of kin notification, Irene said Logan would be devasted by Sarah's death. That he adored his older sister."

"God, I hope they didn't involve him," she said. "Do you know how old he is?"

"I'm not sure. Sarah was nineteen, and he's younger, so maybe fifteen or sixteen," Ethan said. "Why?"

"According to Jessica, an inexperienced driver parked the forklift incorrectly. Maybe Logan is involved," Caitlin replied.

"Shit, I hope not."

"Me too," she said. Then an idea popped into her head. "We need to get a pair of shoes from each person. If they won't cooperate, we'll need a warrant. I'll leave a note for Natalie to work on that in the morning."

"Why? There weren't any visible footprints that we can match the shoes to," Ethan said.

She held up one finger, "Wait a second," then dialed Jessica. "Hi, Jess. Are you free for an hour around noon tomorrow?"

"Sure. Are you buying me lunch?" Jessica asked.

"Not this time. Could you bring Sparky back to the brewery? I have another small job for him."

"What do you have in mind?"

"I'll tell you tomorrow. And can you also be flexible on the time? The timing depends on something I have to do first."

"Of course. Just give me a heads-up if you have to change the time. It takes us about fifteen minutes to get into town from here."

"Will do. Chat tomorrow," Caitlin hung up and looked at Ethan. "I want to see if Sparky can track any scents using the shoes of the Wollman family."

"Track from where to where?"

"Inside the brewery. Primarily from where Olivia was attacked to the kettle, but he'll be free to roam anywhere his nose takes him."

Ethan's face expressed his doubt.

"It was something that Jessica said earlier about Sparky following a scent from the stack of pallets to the kettle. She thought the same person might be involved in both incidents. I ignored her theory at the time, but now I think it's worth investigating further."

"Okay. It's worth a try. Although the staff has probably started the cleanup of the brewery, and Sparky might run into the strong odors of industrial strength cleaners," Ethan said.

"I instructed the owners not to touch *anything* until we release the scene. I hope they listened," she said. "Let's get some sleep, and start again tomorrow morning."

"Sounds good. See you tomorrow," Ethan said and headed for the exit.

Caitlin picked up her jacket and stood in front of the incident board, staring at the photos. She was certain the Wollmans were also responsible for Olivia's injuries, and they had intended to kill her with the stack of pallets.

Not satisfied with their progress on the investigation, she dropped her jacket on the desk and sat down. Typing rapidly, she wrote an email to Natalie asking her to obtain a warrant for all electronic devices plus the three pairs of shoes from the Wollmans, as the scent reference for Sparky. Then she wrote another email to Evan directing him to recheck any CCTV footage from the brewery for any person who resembled either Ed, Irene, or Logan Wollman. She downloaded and attached a social media profile photo of Logan and reminded Natalie that current photos of Irene and Ed were posted on the incident board.

Then she wrote a second email to the owners' group at Cactus Brewing telling them that she would be bringing Sparky in for a second sweep of the brewery and reminding them not to move or clean anything until they released the scene.

"Okay. Maybe now I'll be able to shut my brain off for a few hours of sleep," she said to the empty room.

Chapter 35

Penticton RCMP station

The following morning, Caitlin and Ethan escorted Irene Wollman and Barry Kramer back to the same bland room. Caitlin recited the legal caution statement and then started the interview.

"As I mentioned yesterday evening, we have a few more questions, Mrs. Wollman," Caitlin said.

"Where is my husband? Why isn't he here?" Irene asked, searching with her eyes to the left and then the right as if he was hiding somewhere in the room.

"He's confessed to attacking Noah, and we have to keep his case separate," Ethan explained.

"But, that's my point. Ed has confessed. What more could you possibly want from me?"

"We're also investigating the incident involving Olivia Caponera. Where were you on the afternoon of December 26th?" Caitlin asked.

"At home." She dropped her hands into her lap and squeezed hard to stop the trembling.

"Do you have anyone who can confirm that you were at home?"

"My husband, Ed."

"Anyone else, Mrs. Wollman?"

Her eyes slid sideways. "No one else was home."

"And where was your son?" Caitlin pretended to check her notes, "Logan, is it?"

"Yes, his name is Logan, and he was out with friends. He likes to hang out with his school friends during the holidays and play online action games for hours. I keep telling him to get outside, to get more exercise, but you know teenage boys, always ignoring their moms. He says I nag him too much. Honestly, kids can be exhausting at times." *Stop babbling. Stop it.*

"My son is only a toddler," Ethan spoke up. "I am looking forward to teaching him sports when he's older. How old is Logan now?" He asked.

Caitlin subtly leaned back, letting Ethan take the lead. Empathy was his go-to interviewing technique. Sharing a mutual interest whether it was children, sports, or cars was his method to gain the person's trust.

"He just turned sixteen," Irene answered.

"Has he started driving lessons yet?"

She smiled at Ethan, "Not formally. Ed and I have let him get the feel of driving in the shopping center parking lot, early in the morning before the stores open."

"Gosh, that's early for a teenager. The grocery store opens at seven in the morning," Ethan said.

"We don't go that early. We usually wait until around eight or eight-thirty. The parking lot is still quite empty at that time of the day."

"Is Logan a good driver?"

"He's going to be good. He's smart and has steady hands."

Ethan nodded, and with a tiny motion of his head, indicated that Caitlin should take over the questioning.

"We'll need more than your husband as your alibi, Mrs. Wollman," Caitlin said. "He's been charged with homicide in the case of Noah Atkins. And someone injured Olivia Caponera the day before. They were both at the party where Sarah was given a lethal combination of drugs and alcohol."

"We didn't do it!"

"I can't just take your word for it, Mrs. Wollman. We are presently rechecking the files of the CCTV cameras at the brewery. Are we going to find you and your husband on those files?"

"No, of course not!" Irene said.

"You say you were home on December 26th. We'll need a list of chores, activities, anyone you spoke to, emails sent, or TV programs you watched. Anything to help us confirm that you were home all day," Caitlin said, pushing a legal pad and pen toward the woman.

Irene set her jaw, and pushed the pad right back to Caitlin's side of the table, "I was grieving. I just hid in our bedroom and wept. I don't even remember if I ate anything that day, or the day before."

"I sympathize with you, Mrs. Wollman," Caitlin said, softly. "However, we've sent a car to bring your son in for questioning."

"No! You can't do that! He's only a child."

"He will need a responsible adult to be with him," Caitlin agreed. "Would you like Mr. Kramer to be that adult and his lawyer?"

"It has to be me, no one else."

"I'm sorry, ma'am. You are under suspicion for the attack on Olivia Caponera and Noah Atkins. You won't be allowed to speak to, or text, Logan before we interview him."

"Give me a moment to confer with my client," Kramer said.

"Certainly." For the recording, Caitlin and Ethan verbally signed out and left the room.

"Irene, you need to tell me what's going on," Kramer said.

"They're too lazy to find other suspects, so they are blaming us for everything. We've lost our precious daughter and now they are harassing our son," She put her head in her hands and sobbed.

Kramer lightly laid his hand on her back, "Irene, I don't care if you are guilty or innocent. It's my job to defend you. But, unless I know what I am defending you against, I can't do my job."

She raised her tear-stained face, "What about Logan? He's only a child."

"What did he do?"

"He has a temper, like his dad," she whispered. "I've tried to teach him to channel his anger, but sometimes it overwhelms him."

"What did he do?" Kramer repeated.

"He just went to talk to Olivia at the brewery, to ask her why she was so mean to his sister. He saw her crush out a cigarette, then walk back inside, and he followed her. He said he got angry because she was still alive and his sister was dead. The next thing he knew, the stack of cans fell over and hit Olivia. He said it was an accident."

"How did he manage to push the pallets over? As far as I can remember they each weigh a fair amount."

"He said he used the forklift and shoved the stack."

Kramer quietly inhaled a deep breath. He had heard a lot of things in his career as a lawyer, but this family was inventive. Drowning a young man in a vat of boiling beer. And injuring another person with a stack of wooden pallets and beer cans. "I need to speak with Logan. Are you okay with me being his responsible adult? Or do you have a family member that you would like to bring in as well?"

"I have a sister, who lives in Kamloops," she said, naming a city that was a three-hour drive in optimal conditions. During the winter, the mountain passes could be snowy and fog-shrouded, making the trip slow and treacherous.

"Can you give me her contact information?" Kramer asked.

"No, don't call her! She likes to gossip and she'll tell her friends. I don't want her to destroy Logan's future."

Logan's future looks bleak at the moment. Kramer kept that thought to himself. "Okay. I'm going to speak to Logan. You will be held here until his interview is over. Then we'll see what their next move is."

Irene sagged. "Oh Sarah, my sweet baby girl, why did you go to that terrible party?" she mumbled into her hands. "Why?"

Chapter 36

Penticton RCMP station

Kramer knocked on the door asking the uniformed officer to open it. "Mrs. Wollman will remain in this room while I speak to her son. Where is he?"

"Follow me, sir."

A few feet away, the officer opened a second door, "He's in here sir."

"Thank you. Please inform Corporal Smith and Constable Jones that I am conferring with my new client, Logan Wollman. I'll let them know when we are ready."

"Yes, sir."

Kramer stepped inside and smiled at both the youngster and another police officer. "Constable, I need privacy to speak to my client," he said, gesturing to the door.

"Yes, sir. Do you need anything before I leave?" The young woman asked as she walked toward the door.

Kramer studied the teenager, "Hi Logan. I'm Barry Kramer. Your mom has asked me to help you. Would you like a soda or a bottle of water before we start our chat?"

Under the brim of a ball cap, Logan's red-rimmed eyes briefly met Kramer's, then he dropped his chin, hiding his expression. "No thanks. I'm good."

"Right. We're fine for now, Constable. Thank you."

As the young officer exited, Kramer settled himself in a chair beside Logan and pulled out his legal pad. "How much has your mom told you?"

"Dad is in jail. Mom's here somewhere, being questioned." He nervously adjusted his cap.

"That's basically correct," Kramer agreed. "Your father has been charged in relation to Noah Atkins's death, and he has been transferred to the remand center in Oliver. Your mother is being questioned about the incident with Olivia Caponera. And you will be questioned next. So, please tell me what happened."

"I don't know. I played video games all day with my friends," Logan said, refusing to meet Kramer's eyes.

"No, not what your parents told you to say. Tell me the truth. I am your lawyer, and as I just told your mother, I don't care if you are innocent or guilty. I have to defend you to the very best of my abilities," Kramer stated. "Now, what happened?"

Logan's jaw tightened, "I sort of drove the forklift into the pile of cans and knocked it over onto Olivia."

"Who taught you to drive a forklift?"

"No one. Dad has been teaching me how to drive his truck, and I just figured it out by myself.

Except I wasn't very good with maneuvering the forks, so I just shoved them into the stack and hit the gas."

"Did you intend to hurt her?"

"I don't know. I was really angry," he said. "She's the reason my sister is dead!"

Not wanting to argue whether Olivia was to blame, Kramer asked, "Did you call for help?"

Logan's expression turned stoney, "No."

Kramer stopped himself from telling his client what an absolute shit he was, deliberately abandoning an injured person. "And then what happened."

"Olivia screamed when the cans started hitting her. Then I heard someone running toward me, so I ducked out the back door and ran."

"That's going to be a problem. The police will have CCTV footage of you running away."

With a tiny smirk of pride, Logan said, "They won't find anything. I deleted it from the tapes."

Shocked, Kramer's jaw dropped open. "You what?"

"I hacked into the brewery's cloud storage and deleted the images of me entering and leaving."

"Won't someone notice a glitch in the time stamp?" Kramer asked, wondering if his current knowledge of CCTV systems was valid, or years behind. Technology advanced so quickly, and it was difficult to keep up to date.

"No. I fixed that too."

Sixteen and he knows how to hack a security system and cover his tracks. That's scary. "How did you learn to do that?"

"Friends," Logan answered, vaguely.

"School friends?" Kramer was intrigued.

"Nah. Other friends."

"Do those friends know that you hacked into the brewery's cameras?"

"No," Logan said. *But I told Mom, and she told Dad.*

"Then what did you do?"

"I called Dad. Told him I had been hanging out with friends in town, and I needed a ride home," Logan said. "He said he'd come get me."

"What time was that?"

"No idea. A few minutes after I left the brewery."

"Where did he pick you up?"

"In the park. Near the art gallery."

"Did you tell your dad what happened?"

"Of course not," he said, with a surly twitch of his lips.

"Why not?"

"I wasn't sure how he would react."

"Then what happened?"

"Nothing. We ate dinner, watched a movie and then I went to bed."

221

"And your parents? What did they do?"

"Same. We had dinner and watched a movie together. I didn't hear them come upstairs, so I must have fallen asleep before they went to bed." *They shouted and argued for hours, trying to decide what to do, and in the end, they didn't do anything.*

Kramer flicked back to the notes he had taken during Irene's interview with Corporal Smith.

Irene: I was grieving. I just hid in our bedroom and wept. I don't even remember if I ate anything that day, or the day before.

"Logan, that doesn't match with what your mom just told the police."

"What did she say?"

"That's not how this works. You tell me what happened, and I figure out how to defend you."

"I'm not saying anything more until I talk to Mom."

"That won't happen until after the police have interviewed her," Kramer said. "I'm on your side, son. I'm here to defend you."

"I'm not your son, and my dad is in jail. I want to talk to my mom," he said, angrily.

"Your mom said you have an aunt in Kamloops. Would you like me to contact her? It could take a few hours for her to get here, and you'll have to stay at the police station until she arrives, but I can call her for you," Kramer said.

"No! Keep her out of this. Mom will know what to do."

"Logan, you are only sixteen. If both of your parents are charged and held in the remand center, you will need an adult to be responsible for you."

"What? No. You can't take both of my parents."

"I'm not taking them. Your dad confessed to contributing to Noah's death. He is being held until his bail hearing. Your mom is being questioned, and unless she can convince the police that she didn't harm either Noah or Olivia, she could also be detained," he said, bluntly stating the worst possible outcome. "Now, please give me your aunt's contact information. It will take her a few hours to get here."

"I don't have it."

"You know her name."

Logan glared at Kramer, "Tina."

"Last name?"

"Fellows."

"Husband?"

"Denis."

"Street?" He asked, controlling his growing impatience.

"I'm not sure."

"I can find them without the address, but it would be simpler if you cooperated."

"Fine. Laurier Drive, and before you ask, I don't know the house number or their phone number."

"Thank you. I have to go back to the interview with your mom. Do you need to use the men's room? Or do you want a bottle of water?"

"No."

"There will be an officer in the room, or just outside the door if you need anything," Kramer stood and shoved his notepad into his briefcase. "Just stay calm, Logan. Put your head down on the table, and snooze if you can. This could take a while."

Kramer tapped on the door, "I'm finished for now. My client is underage, and cannot be interviewed until he has a responsible adult with him. I am going to contact his aunt. Please try to keep him comfortable in the meantime."

"Yes, sir," the woman replied.

Kramer headed for the men's room, before returning to the room where Irene was waiting. This was shaping up to be a long day.

Before he re-entered the room where Irene was being held, he quickly called his assistant. Reciting Tina Fellows' details, he explained he needed Logan's aunt, to come to Penticton. He instructed his assistant to be firm. "Give enough details that she won't waffle, but get her here today."

Chapter 37

Cactus Brewing

Caitlin spotted Jessica waiting in her Jeep at the front entrance. She waved, then walked toward her.

Jessica opened the driver's door and stepped out, with Sparky on her heels. "What's this mysterious job you have for us?"

"And hello to you too," Caitlin said.

"Hello, how are you? Lovely day isn't it," Jessica replied, dryly. "What's up?"

"I'd like Sparky to smell some shoes." It had been a hard sell, but she had been able to convince a judge that she had probable cause for a limited warrant allowing her to remove the three pairs of shoes from the Wollman home and any electronic devices. She held up three separate evidence bags, each labeled with a number, but no names. She didn't want the names of their suspects known to anyone but her team. "Let's go around to the back entrance."

Jessica jiggled Sparky's leash, "Come on pooch. We have a job for you."

As they walked, Caitlin said, "You mentioned the other day that you thought Sparky could separate and track multiple scents. Is that true? Or were you just blowing smoke?"

"A properly trained dog can sort out what he or she is supposed to find, and ignore everything else. Sparky hasn't been formally trained, as you have kindly pointed out on several occasions," she said, softening her sardonic comment with a ghost of a smile. "But I believe in his extraordinary nose."

"Alright, let's see if he is as talented as you say he is," Caitlin knocked on the rear door, and Rhys poked his head out.

"Right on time," he said, opening the door, fully.

"Hi Rhys. Do you know Jessica?" Caitlin asked.

"Yep. Hi Jess," he said and bent to give Sparky a butt scratch. "And how are you doing little man?"

"Hi Rhys, it's good to see you. How are you coping?" Jessica asked. His eyes were sunken, and underlined by dark circles.

"Coping," he replied, not mentioning his sleepless nights, nightmares, poor appetite, and a few drinks. "So, how can I help?"

"First, can you confirm that nothing has been cleaned at the brewery since you discovered Noah's body?" Caitlin asked.

The memory of Noah's boiled body flooded his brain, and fighting the overwhelming urge to puke, he nodded curtly. "Nothing has changed."

"Good," Caitlin set the three plastic bags on a stack of empty cans that hadn't been involved in the original incident. She selected one, opened it, and then lowered the bag to Sparky's height. "Jess, can you do your magic and get this guy to sniff the shoes and then see if he does anything?"

"Sure, but it would be easier if I could hold the bag for him."

"Wait one second while I photograph the evidence number so that we can keep track," Caitlin said, then handed the bag to Jessica.

Being careful not to touch the shoes, Jessica opened the bag wider and lowered it under Sparky's nose. "Buscar, Sparky. Buscar."

Rhys shot Caitlin a questioning look, whispering, "Buscar?"

"Buscar means search. He's our bilingual investigative consultant," she replied with a straight face. "I'm going to video his route," she said, as she activated the camera on her phone.

Sparky's nose dropped to the concrete, skimming so close to the surface that he left a trail of wet nose prints. His body trembled with the force of his deep inhaling and exhaling. Walking slowly to the area where Olivia had been attacked, he circled the area several times, his tail flapping furiously, then he crossed the brewhouse to the kettle. He stopped at the stairs leading to the hatch and sat looking up. He still refused to climb the perforated metal stairway.

"Good job, Sparky. Good job," Jessica said, rewarding him with a brisk scratch on his rump.

"That's similar to the path that he tracked after Noah was discovered," Caitlin said, avoiding the words murder and killed.

"What do you think that means?" Rhys asked.

"The owner of those shoes probably was inside the brewery and walked from the spot where Olivia was attacked, to the kettle where Noah was attacked," Jessica said, belatedly noticing Caitlin's annoyed expression for revealing the information. "At least that's what I think, but I could be wrong."

Caitlin ignored Jessica's attempt to backtrack from her oversharing and made a note on her phone. *First set of shoes: Ed Wollman.*

"How can you be so sure?" Rhys asked.

Jessica shrugged, "Not certain enough that I'd swear on a stack of Bibles in court, but from everything I've read, and from watching my pooch interact with scents, I'm sure he's got it right. Dogs smell between 10,000 to 100,000 times better than people, and they can detect odors in parts per trillion. That's like a dog finding one dirty sock in a pile of two million clean ones."

"Jessica," Caitlin shook her head, slightly.

"Sorry. I'm running my mouth."

"Can we try the second set of shoes? Or will that confuse him?" Caitlin asked.

Jessica looked down at Sparky, "I'm pretty sure he'll be fine. Let's see what happens." She returned Sparky to the same starting point, took the second bag from Caitlin then let him smell the shoes. "Buscar, Sparky. Buscar."

He was slower to react, zig-zagging slowly across the floor, trying to find the scent.

"Maybe it is too confusing for him to search for a second scent?" Caitlin said, following him with the camera app on her phone.

"Or the owner of the shoes wasn't here recently," Jessica replied. "Wait, he's got it. See his tail? He does two rapid beats to the right, and one to the left when he's got the scent."

Sparky followed the trail to the bottom of the metal stairway, and once again sat at the bottom looking up.

Jessica gave him more pats and butt scratches. "Good boy. Such a good boy."

"Why don't you give him treats when he does a good job?" Rhys asked.

"He likes butt scratches better than treats."

Caitlin checked the video. "He didn't spend a lot of time where Olivia was attacked. What do you think that means?" Caitlin asked, she'd given up trying to keep information from Rhys. *Second set of shoes: Irene Wollman.*

"Just a guess. He didn't find much of anything over there. The scent was stronger on this side, by the kettle."

"Okay to try the third set?"

"Yep, let's give it a go," Jessica replied, repeating the process once again. "Buscar, Sparky. Buscar."

He skimmed the concrete, heading almost immediately from the back door to the area where

Olivia had been buried by the pallets and cans, then changed directions and sought out the forklift which was parked off to one side. He circled it twice, then sat beside the vehicle, his tail bouncing. Right. Right. Left. And repeat.

Jessica patted him, and looked at Caitlin, "Can I set him inside the forklift?"

Caitlin hesitated. *Had the FIS team processed the forklift?* "Give me a few minutes. I have to check something." She rapidly tapped the numbers, "Ethan. Can you quickly check something and call me back?"

"Sure. What do you need?"

"I'm at Cactus Brewing with Jessica and Sparky. Did FIS process the forklift?"

"Hold on, it will just take a minute to check."

Five minutes later, Ethan replied, "Yes. It's been done. Has your theory worked out?"

"I'll fill you in when I get back to the detachment," Caitlin said and abruptly disconnected the call. "Jess, it's okay to lift Sparky into the forklift," she said.

Jessica scooped him up, one hand across his chest just behind his front legs, and the other hand around his butt, and set him on the floor of the forklift. His tail bounced enthusiastically, indicating he was smelling the scent more strongly. "I'd say contestant number three could have been the person who used the forklift on December 26th."

"Contestant number three?" Caitlin huffed a quick laugh while making notes on her phone. *Third set of shoes: Logan Wollman. Stronger scent inside the forklift.* As soon as they finished here, she'd follow up on the fingerprint reports.

And that brought another question to mind, "Hey, Jess, why didn't Sparky 'hit' on the forklift when he was sniffing around after Olivia's accident?"

"Because he was searching for a human. That was his priority," Jessica replied.

"Understood," Caitlin said.

"However, he did show interest in the forklift, but he didn't have a reference scent so he wouldn't have focused on only one," Jessica said. "Now he knows which scents he is supposed to find," she said, as her pooch jumped out of the forklift and speedily followed an invisible path straight to the kettle, his tail bouncing out his message.

I smell that person here, too.

Intrigued, Jessica asked Caitlin, "Just to confirm the three sets of shoes are from three different people, right?"

"Yes."

"Are any of them from the employees or owners?"

"You know I can't give you that information."

"Sparky has indicated that all three people have used this stairway or been close to the kettle," Jessica said. "That includes employees, or the owners, who might legitimately be here, or the assailants who shouldn't be. Unless the assailants *are* employees or owners," she added softly, sending a worried look at Rhys.

Rhys quickly stepped out of his shoes and offered them to Jessica. "See if he gets a hit off of mine. Anyone working here could have been in the same area in the past few weeks. Maybe Sparky is getting too much information."

She reached for Rhys's shoes, and looked at Caitlin, "Is this okay with you?"

"Sure. Let's see what happens."

"Okay, come on Sparky. Let's go back to the start and make this test as consistent as possible," she said and then repeated the same sequence.

Caitlin and Rhys looked on, while Jessica trailed after Sparky, keeping an eye on him. This time he was slower, minutely examining all areas of the brewery. Several times his tail signaled an area saturated with Rhys's scent including the stairway that he had hit on for the three other tests.

Rhys nodded in agreement each time. "Yep. My duties take me all over the brewery, including to the second-floor mezzanine, in the coolers, at the canning line, in the lab, and occasionally the taproom. He seems to have zeroed in on my scent. I am impressed."

"It is impressive," Caitlin agreed. "But, because Sparky isn't an officially trained scent dog, it won't stand up in court."

"Was this a waste of time, then?" Jessica asked.

"No, not at all. It will help us search for solid evidence," Caitlin said. Her mind kept scratching at something Rhys had said. "Rhys, can you repeat what you just said?"

"I said, I'm impressed with Sparky."

"No, before that. You listed the various areas of the brewery. Repeat that."

"Okay, the production floor, administration mezzanine, coolers, canning line, laboratory, and sometimes the taproom."

"What areas are too noisy for you to hear what's happening out here?"

"Every process in a brewery is noisy," he exhaled loudly. "Grinding the grain, operating the canning line, or when we run the centrifuge, then it's so loud in here it's hard to think. Even the kettle is loud. When the burners kick in, it sounds a bit like a hot air balloon about to take off."

"On the 27th, which of those operations were happening?"

"Grinding the grain. Noah and I worked on that, together. Then the brewing started before lunch," Rhys said. "I lost track of him between adding the first hops and the last hops at four-thirty. I can't be more specific than that."

"Any soundproof areas?" Caitlin asked.

"The cold room is insulated and quieter, and the lab is tucked away on the mezzanine away from the main flow of work."

She chewed the inside of her cheek. "Were you in any of those areas on the 27th?"

"Definitely the lab."

"Approximately what time?"

"I typically spend an hour running tests on the various stages of our brews to confirm everything is doing what it's supposed to be doing," he looked down, mentally reviewing his work day. "I'm fairly sure I was in the lab from about three until four in the afternoon."

"Do you remember seeing Noah during that time?"

"No, I don't remember seeing him."

"What about after four?"

Rhys looked stricken. "No," he quietly replied. "Was he already in the kettle by then? Was there something I could have done to save him?"

"I'm trying to pinpoint the time of the incident," she said. "And even if he was already in the kettle while you were here, I don't think you could have saved him. He wouldn't have lasted long at that temperature."

"I feel terrible," he said. "I thought that he'd left early without telling me, or he was hiding somewhere in the brewery and avoiding the cleanup duties. I was too angry to go looking for him so I checked on the brew, and signed out for the night. I planned to ask him the next morning what he had been doing."

"You can't keep beating yourself up, Rhys. You had no way of knowing." Jessica said.

"Do you have someone you can talk to?" Caitlin asked.

"I'm fine."

"I've seen a lot of gruesome stuff in this job, and I make sure I get professional help after events like this," Caitlin said.

"I hear you," he said half-heartedly.

Chapter 38

Penticton RCMP station

Kramer stepped into the room where Irene was waiting impatiently.

"Irene, this is going to take a while longer. Would you like a sandwich? Or a bottle of water? Anything?"

She held her stomach as if she was in pain. "No food, just water."

Kramer dug a twenty-dollar bill out of his pocket and handed it to the officer, glancing at her name tag, "Constable Olsen, do you think you could bring me something from the vending machine? A sandwich would be great, but I'll take anything available. And two bottles of water, please."

"I'll be right back," Olsen said.

Kramer set his briefcase on the table and took a moment to stretch his body, twisting from side to side, and rotating his shoulders. He caught Irene staring at him. "It helps revive my circulation and increase my concentration."

She didn't reply.

Olsen rapped on the door and opened it. "Here you go, sir. The label says turkey and cheese, but it looks like mystery meat to me," she said, handing him the food and his change, then set the bottles on the table.

He grinned at her description, "It will fill the hole in my stomach. Thank you. Please let Corporal Smith know that we should be ready to start again shortly. I just need to speak to Mrs. Wollman alone for a few minutes."

"Will do. Just tap on the door when you are ready to continue."

He peeled back the plastic cover and sniffed cautiously. "Seems okay, are you sure you couldn't eat half, Irene?"

She grimaced and shook her head. "No, thank you."

"I just need five minutes to inhale this, and then we need to talk before resuming the interview," he said, taking a large bite. He chewed briefly, swallowed, and took another big bite. "It's not pretty when I eat. There is never enough time to savor the flavors although this doesn't have much in the way of flavor to savor." In less than five minutes, he tossed the empty plastic wrapper in a garbage can and drank the last mouthful of water.

"Let's get back to it, then." He flipped his pad to a fresh page and eyed Irene. "We have a problem. Logan's account of the stack of cans falling on Olivia is dramatically different from yours. I need you to be straight with me."

She jerked upright, "what did he say? He's only a child. He wouldn't remember the details."

"Logan said he drove the forklift into the stack of cans and pallets. He also said that he hacked into and altered the security camera footage. He was quite specific about his actions."

"No. That's not what happened." Irene shook her head forcefully. "He's covering for his dad."

"I'm confused. Are you saying that Ed was involved in the attack on Olivia?" Kramer asked.

"What? No! I thought you were talking about Noah," she said, quickly backpedaling.

"I was talking about Olivia. Was Ed in the brewery when she was injured?" Kramer watched Irene struggle with the answer as if she was contemplating saying yes, that Ed had attacked both of the victims.

"I'm tired and confused." She finally said, "I haven't slept since...Sarah."

"I understand," Kramer said. Not satisfied with her answer, he tried a different angle. "Did Ed use the forklift to hoist Noah into the kettle?" he asked, trying to visualize how an unconscious body could be manhandled into the kettle.

Averting her head, she mumbled, "No."

"Did Logan?"

"Don't be ridiculous. He wasn't there when Noah died," she replied, turning her head to squarely meet his questioning look. *Logan had told her that he'd somehow accessed the cameras and deleted the files in the cloud bank or something like that. Had he done it properly?*

"The police will have processed everything at the brewery for fibers and fingerprints. It shouldn't take much longer for them to identify whoever drove the forklift. It's better if you don't lie when responding to a question that they already know the answer to. Do you understand?"

"Fine," she sighed. "Logan told me he was driving the forklift and he accidentally knocked over the stack of cans."

"He told me it wasn't an accident. That he deliberately pushed the stack onto Olivia," Kramer countered.

"That's not what happened!"

"Irene, is Ed protecting Logan?"

Her jaw went slack then she quickly recovered. "No, it happened just like Ed told you. He hit Noah, and put him in the kettle."

"If Logan's prints are anywhere near or on the kettle, the investigation into Noah's death will focus on him," Kramer said.

Ignoring Kramer's statement, she blurted, "They said they had a search warrant for our shoes. What does that mean?"

"Who said that?" Kramer demanded, startled by this new piece of information.

"That woman cop, the redhead. She showed it to me while you were talking to Logan."

"Corporal Smith? She had a warrant for your shoes?"

"Yes."

"The shoes you were wearing on December 27th?"

"She didn't say. She also wanted a house key and the alarm code."

"Bloody hell," Kramer muttered. "I have to find out what's going on. By the way, your sister Tina should be here in a few hours, to be Logan's responsible adult."

"What? No, I told you not to call her," her hand flew up to cover her mouth.

"We had no choice, Irene. Logan needs an adult with him in the interview, and you and Ed are not available."

"Why can't you be the adult?"

"It is in his best interest to have a family member available. That would allow me to concentrate on defending him. Now, I'm going to step outside, and find out what is going on with that search warrant," he said, then rapped on the door.

"Ready so soon, sir?"

"I need to speak to Corporal Smith, privately. Where is she?"

Olsen replied, "She's executing a search warrant, sir."

"Exactly. I didn't know about the search warrant until Mrs. Wollman informed me. That's unacceptable."

"Do you have her phone number, sir?"

"Yes."

"That would be the quickest way to reach her."

Kramer bit back a curse and walked a distance away from the interview rooms. *Why the hell did Smith want shoes from the entire Wollman family?* He jabbed the numbers on his phone and paced while it rang.

Caitlin saw Kramer's name pop up on an incoming call. "Good afternoon, Mr. Kramer," she said.

"Why didn't you tell me about the search warrant?"

"I spoke to your client, Mrs. Wollman."

"Why do you need the shoes from the entire Wollman family?" he demanded.

"We have reason to believe that some of the family members are involved in both incidents."

"What proof do you have?"

"We are expecting the fingerprint report to confirm who used the forklift during the attack on Olivia, and who put Noah in the kettle." She said, looking at the three pairs of shoes in the plastic bags. She couldn't tell him about Sparky following the scent tracks. He'd have that quashed, immediately.

"Then why do you need their shoes?"

"It's another lead we are following."

"I am not happy with this stunt, Corporal Smith," Kramer said. He had no idea what Smith was up to, but it sure as hell didn't feel right. "We're ready to conclude Irene's interview. She has a teenage son who needs her," he said, with a hint of bravado, as if Irene could leave whenever she chose.

"I will be there in less than ten minutes," Caitlin assured Kramer and disconnected the call. "That was fun," she muttered.

"Are we done then?" Jessica asked as she walked with Caitlin toward their cars.

"Sorry, wait one minute while I get this," she said, answering a call from Ethan. "Ethan, anything from FIS on the fingerprints?"

"Not yet," Ethan said.

"Pressure them. We need that information."

"Working on it," Ethan said. "I have some not-great news."

"Now what?" She asked.

"Evan says the CCTV video from the brewery has been damaged."

"The video is damaged for both incidents, Olivia's and Noah's?"

"Yes."

"How could that happen?" Caitlin asked.

"He's not sure, but it appears to have a glitch. It's choppy."

"Shit. Then we need those fingerprints. ASAP," she said, turning her head slightly, annoyance flicked in her eyes when she realized Jessica and Sparky were still standing beside her cruiser. She waved a perfunctory goodbye, opened the driver's door, and slid inside.

"What did you find at the brewery?" Ethan asked.

Confirming that Jessica was walking away, she said to Ethan, "Listen with an open mind, okay?"

"Okay."

"I had Sparky smell each pair of shoes from the Wollman's. He was able to track their scents through the brewery to the kettle and the forklift. Logan's scent was strongest in the forklift, and where Olivia was attacked, but it is also strong near the kettle. I think Ed confessed to protect his son."

"Can we prove it?"

"We need that fingerprint report ASAP. Sparky's tracking won't stand up as evidence because he's not a registered tracker."

"I'll call FIS right now," Ethan said. "But, for comparison, we only have Ed Wollman's prints on file. And we can't fingerprint or photograph Logan until we charge him."

"And we can't charge Logan, at the moment," Caitlin said, "until we can prove that he was involved."

"Yep, it's a Catch-22."

"However," Caitlin said, "Barry Kramer called me a few minutes ago, and they are ready to resume the interview with Irene. She has already admitted that she was in the brewery when her husband attacked Noah. At a minimum, she is an accessory after the fact and that will give us her prints," Caitlin said.

"Are you headed back to the station?"

"Yes."

"If you took a slight detour through Starbucks for lattes, it could give me another five minutes to get the fingerprint report," he said, hopefully.

Caitlin chuckled, "and a brownie?"

"Affirmative."

Chapter 39

Penticton RCMP station

Caitlin parked the cruiser and gathered the two coffees and goodies. Not exactly a nutritious meal, but it would have to do for now. Heading for the squad room, she plunked the food in front of Ethan. "Get that inside you," she chinned in the direction of the coffee and brownie.

"Logan is waiting for his aunt to arrive from Kamloops, to be his responsible adult," Ethan took a bite of the brownie, chewed briefly, and swallowed. "Kramer won't let us interview Logan until she arrives."

"Anything yet on the fingerprints?"

"Yes. Confirmation that Ed Wollman was at the brewery. There is a palm print on the aluminum railing. Lots of other prints not yet identified."

"We should ask the brewery owners and staff for elimination prints," she said between bits of brownie and gulps of hot coffee.

"Let's see what shakes out with Irene, first. Fingerprinting a group is time-consuming, and it can be very upsetting for them," Ethan replied.

"We can assure them that the non-essential fingerprints will be destroyed once we've charged a suspect."

"Still, no one likes to think that they might be implicated by accident."

"Okay, we'll hold off until we've finished with Irene, and Logan." Caitlin stood, "I have to hit the ladies' room, and then I'm ready."

"Same," Ethan also stood and tossed their trash in a nearby garbage can.

"You're going to join me in the *ladies'* room?" Caitlin asked, putting more emphasis on ladies.

"Yes, do you have a problem with that?" he asked.

Caitlin's laughter followed him as he pushed open the door to the men's room.

A few minutes later, Caitlin and Ethan knocked and then entered the interview room. "Good afternoon, Irene. I'm glad you are ready to resume our conversation."

"I don't have much choice, do I? I have to get this over with so that I can be with my underage son," she said bitterly.

"Our understanding is your sister is on her way from Kamloops to be with Logan," Ethan said.

"She's hopeless in a crisis. I need to be with my son."

"Alright, let's proceed, and see if we can reunite you with Logan," Caitlin said, dangling the carrot in front of Irene. She nodded at Ethan to start the recording and then she recited the necessary formal statement.

Kramer spoke up immediately, "What did you remove from the Wollman home without my knowledge?"

His aggressive stance wasn't unexpected, and Caitlin responded calmly. "As per our search warrant, we removed personal electronic devices, and one pair of shoes per person."

"Why the shoes?"

"We need them for comparison," Caitlin hedged.

"Why?"

"We believe that Logan drove the forklift, causing Olivia's injuries," not exactly how she had intended this to go, but now it was out there.

"What proof do you have?"

"That's what the shoes will confirm," she said, hoping that Kramer would think shoeprints and not scents.

"Logan said it was an accident!" Irene blurted.

"Irene! Stop talking. Let me do my job," Kramer said, forcefully.

Silently Caitlin cheered. It was the opening she needed. Irene had now implicated both herself and Logan giving Caitlin cause to detain both of them, and take their fingerprints and a DNA sample. Irene had blurted the same tired excuse, 'It was an accident' when her husband confessed to striking Noah. She really should listen to her lawyer.

Ignoring Kramer, Irene continued to ramble. "He's just a kid. He was distraught that Olivia was responsible for Sarah's death. We didn't know he had done it until he told us at dinner that night."

"Mrs. Wollman, are you saying your son admitted to harming Olivia Caponera?"

"Yes," she whispered. "And he is very sorry for hurting her."

Kramer's face registered anger, and then a resentful surrender to the inevitable. "Corporal Smith, we need to discuss mitigating circumstances for Logan. As Mrs. Wollman has pointed out, Logan is a minor, who is suffering greatly over the loss of his only, and beloved, sister. I think we could sort out this misunderstanding without going to trial. Perhaps a stint of community hours to atone for his poor judgment?"

"We are charging Mrs. Wollman with aiding and abetting. She knew her son caused Olivia's injuries and she has been protecting him," Caitlin said. She will be processed, fingerprinted, and held over for her bail hearing."

"Wait," Kramer patted the air. "Please don't detain both parents. Logan is underage."

"His aunt will be here shortly. She can be his legal guardian," Caitlin said.

Staring silently at Caitlin for a moment, Kramer couldn't decide if she was naturally a hard-ass, or if she found solid evidence at the brewery linking Logan to this case, and perhaps to the death of Noah Atkins. "Corporal Smith before you formally charge Irene, may I have five minutes with her?"

"Yes," Caitlin said, motioning to Ethan to sign out, and then they left the room.

Kramer turned to Irene, "You have to let me do my job, Irene. You lied to the police. You know that Olivia's injuries were not an accident. You can't perjure yourself for your son."

"Of course, I can," she said, coldly. "I will testify that he was crying hysterically when he returned home. That this was a terrible accident. He doesn't know how to properly drive a forklift," she said. "If anything, I think the brewery owners are legally responsible for Olivia's injuries. The forklift was just sitting there, with the keys in it and available to anyone."

"Logan did not have a legitimate reason to be in the employees-only area of the brewery or to drive their forklift. He is not trained, and he is not an employee of the brewery," Kramer said, making a note, to not put her on the stand. She thought she could help her son by lying.

"It's the truth. He told me it was an accident." She mulishly set her jaw.

Kramer inhaled deeply, then exhaled slowly. "We also need to engage two more lawyers, Irene. I can't represent the three of you. It's a conflict of interest."

"Fine, but I want to interview them, to see if they understand the situation properly," she said.

"Who do you want me to represent?" Kramer asked, unsure if he was about to be released from representing any of the family.

"Take care of my baby boy. He's all I have left."

"Alright. While you are being processed, I'll stay with Logan and find lawyers for you and Ed," Kramer said. Irene Wollman appeared to be willing to sacrifice her husband for her son. *Things could get ugly.*

Chapter 40

Penticton RCMP station

Standing in the hallway, Kramer sent a text to his assistant, asking her to contact two additional lawyers for the Wollmans. He sent her a short list of names that he felt would be a good fit for either Irene or Ed.

Her reply pinged back. *Got it.*

Then he turned to Constable Olsen and said, "I'll wait with Logan for his aunt to arrive from Kamloops."

"Yes, sir." She unlocked the door and stood aside.

"Hey, Logan. How are you holding up?" Kramer asked as the door swung closed behind him.

The teen stood, stretching his arms overhead. "Is this going to take much longer?"

"We're waiting for your aunt to arrive," Kramer said. "As soon as she gets here, I'll brief her, then we have another interview, and if everything goes well, you'll be released into your aunt's care," he said.

He would have to tell Logan that his mother had implicated him in Olivia Caponera's case when she said that Logan didn't know how to drive a forklift and that he had accidentally caused the

251

stacks to topple. Instead of helping Logan, she had given the police cause to fingerprint him and take a DNA sample and he was certain that would happen as soon as Logan's next interview was completed. Logan's chances of going home tonight were slim. Instead, he would probably be remanded to juvenile custody until his trial.

"Can we get some food while we wait for my aunt? Maybe a pizza or something? And a soda?" Logan asked."

"Sure, let me see what I can do," Kramer said.

Thirty minutes later, Logan wiped the pizza grease from his hands and downed the last of his soda. He burped quietly, then leaned back in the metal chair, and gave Kramer an accessing look. "You are my lawyer, right?"

"Yes. I'm arranging for two other lawyers to represent your mom and your dad. It's better to keep the defense strategies separate."

"So, I can tell you anything, and you can't repeat it to the police? Sort of like a Catholic confessing to a priest."

"Yes, that's right. It's called attorney-client privilege," Kramer replied. "What would you like to tell me?"

"I did it."

Caught off-guard, Kramer's face registered surprise and confusion. "Did what exactly?"

"I flubbed the attempt on Olivia. But I was successful with Noah."

"Logan, are you saying that you deliberately attacked Olivia Caponera?"

"Yeah, but it was my first time driving a forklift. I didn't do a good job of knocking over the cans. I couldn't figure out how to operate the forks properly."

"Why did you do it?"

A deep red flush swept over his face and his voice tightened with anger. "Sarah would still be alive if Olivia hadn't forced her to drive them to that stupid party!"

"To be fair, Logan, Olivia didn't force Sarah. She asked Sarah to go with them."

"Sarah wanted so badly for those stuck-up bitches to like her that she'd do anything they asked."

"Are you also admitting that it was you who attacked Noah Atkins? Not your father?" Kramer asked.

"Yes. Mom made him take the blame," Logan said. "Losing Sarah has been really tough on Mom, and she didn't want to lose me too."

Ignoring Logan's attempt to deflect responsibility, Kramer asked, "Why did you kill Noah?"

"Because Mom said he just sat there and watched my sister die."

Unwilling to interrupt Logan's confession, Kramer didn't argue that according to the police,

Noah was asleep and unaware that Sarah was in trouble.

Instead, he asked, "Logan, how did you kill Noah?"

"I whacked him on the back of his head with that paddle thing, then I used the forklift to lift him up to the hatch and we stuffed him inside."

"We? Who helped you?" Kramer asked.

"My dad."

"I'm unclear on the sequence of events," Kramer said. "How did both you and your dad end up at the brewery?"

"The three of us had a big argument over what happened with Olivia. When they realized that I had left the house, they were worried that I was headed back to the brewery to finish the job. They got there just after I had hit Noah, and Dad helped me stuff his body into the kettle," he replied.

"Why did you put Noah in the kettle?"

"That was Mom's idea. She thought we could get away with it if the body wasn't discovered right away," Logan said.

"Why did your dad confess to something he didn't do?" Kramer asked.

"Mom said she was worried that the cops were going to focus on me. She told Dad he had to confess to keep me out of jail."

"Logan, Noah wasn't dead. He was unconscious."

The teen looked shocked for a few seconds, then he shrugged, "That boiling liquid would have finished him off pretty quickly."

"Don't you feel any remorse?" Kramer asked, horrified at Logan's response.

"No! I'm furious that Olivia survived."

Kramer was speechless. He'd never experienced this depth of raw rage in a sixteen-year-old boy.

"One more question," Logan said. "Can I answer, no comment, to their questions?"

"You can, but it is my job to advise you when and how to safely answer a question," Kramer said.

"I'm going to use it as my standard answer. Then I won't accidentally say something that I shouldn't."

"Logan, this isn't a TV police drama. Answering no comment won't…" Kramer said as a knock on the door interrupted him. He looked up and saw Constable Olsen motioning that she wanted to enter. Waving her inside, he asked, "What can we do for you, constable?"

"Logan's aunt, Tina Fellows, has arrived."

"Show her in please," Kramer said, standing to greet the woman and introduce himself.

He spent twenty minutes explaining the situation to Tina, omitting Logan's recent, attorney-client confession.

Tina's demeanor progressed through several stages of annoyance, shock, and stunned silence as Kramer explained the seriousness of the murder charges against Ed, plus the aiding and abetting charges for Irene.

"What now?" Tina quietly asked.

"The police are waiting to interview Logan," Kramer said.

Kramer tapped on the door, and Constable Olsen opened it. "Please tell the officers that we are ready to proceed," he said.

Olsen nodded, shut, and relocked the door. A few minutes later Caitlin Smith and Ethan Jones entered the room and introduced themselves to the aunt.

"Please, have a seat," Caitlin said, "and we'll get started."

Everyone in the room identified themselves for the recording, and Caitlin asked the first question.

"Can you confirm that your name is Logan Wollman?"

"Yes."

"And you live at..." She recited his address.

"Yes," he said, agreeing with the information.

"Your mother, Irene Wollman, has stated under oath that you drove the forklift on December 26th, and knocked over the stack of pallets and cans onto Olivia Caponera. Is this true?"

"No comment." Logan's response to the next dozen questions was a determined. 'No comment.'

Frustrated, Caitlin signaled to Ethan that he should take over and try his kid-friendly technique.

"Let's see if we can clear up a few details, Logan, and get you back in your home tonight. What do you say?" Ethan said.

"No comment."

"Perhaps it would be better if Logan could get a good sleep, and a proper meal," Kramer suggested. "It's been a long and tiring day for everyone."

Not willing to allow the teen to leave without being fingerprinted, Caitlin said, "Logan Wollman, we are arresting you on suspicion of assault on Olivia Caponera. You will be processed, fingerprinted, and photographed before you are released into the custody of your aunt Tina Fellows. Do you understand?"

He glared at her. "No comment."

Chapter 41

Behind Cactus Brewing

The next day, Jessica parked the Jeep near the brewery and hooked Sparky's lead to his collar, "Come on, pooch. I want to snoop around." She stepped out and waited for Sparky to hop down, then used the remote to lock the doors.

Revolving slowly in a 360-degree turn, she surveyed the buildings. She was standing between the main entrance for Cactus Brewing and a service alley. She couldn't see any security cameras, but that wasn't the view that she was interested in anyway. She tugged Sparky's leash, pulling his attention away from a thorough examination of the base of a power pole and its numerous stinky messages.

Reluctantly, he let her lead him away.

Jessica walked to the back of the building and studied the area. She turned left into the alley, and ambled slowly, allowing Sparky to stop and examine numerous liquid messages deposited on power poles, shrubs, and tall clumps of grass.

It was her habit when mulling over a problem to share her thoughts with Sparky, "I only see one house with an entrance off of this lane." On the off chance that Sparky was paying attention, she pointed her finger at the gate. "That one. Let's take a snoop and see if they have one of those video doorbells."

Standing at the gate, she examined the house.

The back door opened and an older man stepped out. "Can I help you?" He asked, his voice tinged with suspicion.

"Good morning. I'm Jessica and this is my dog, Sparky. I'm sorry to bother you," she said.

"What can I do for you?" The man asked without introducing himself.

"I was wondering if this side of your house has a security camera?"

"Why would you want to know that?"

"Oh God. That sounds creepy, doesn't it? My car was damaged a few nights ago, and I was hoping someone had a camera that recorded the incident." *Lies, lies, lies.*

He scratched his thick white beard, studying her. "Did you report the damage to the police?"

"Yes. But they say they can't do anything unless I know who caused it," she said, mentally crossing her fingers in hopes that her lie wouldn't be discovered.

"I have a security system," he said.

"That's great. Before I go back to the police, can I ask one more question?"

"You can ask," he said, "and I might answer."

"Is the footage stored in the cloud? Or does it get recorded over after a certain amount of time?"

"It's in the cloud."

"That's just what I need. I'll head over to the police station right now, and let them know that I might have proof," she said. "May I have your contact information so that they can arrange to pick up a copy?"

He didn't answer immediately, then said, "Just a minute," and went back inside.

"Come on buddy, don't let me down," she whispered.

He reappeared and walked to the gate. "You are a very determined person, aren't you?" He said, handing her his business card.

Laughing, Jessica said, "If you mean a pain in the ass, yes, I've been told that, several times." She read his card, "Thank you so much, Paul. If any of my less annoying friends need a plumber, I'll be sure to pass your name along."

He finally cracked a small smile. "You do that."

"I'm headed to the police station right now. Hopefully, someone will contact you today for that security footage."

"Don't hold your breath. A scratched car isn't high on their priority list."

"I gotta try! Thanks again," she said, with a wave.

"Sure," Paul replied with a casual flap of his hand. An indifferent wave goodbye.

Urging Sparky back in the direction of the Jeep, she said, "It's a good thing he can't see our vehicle. Then he'd know I'm a big fat liar."

Sparky ignored her comments and pulled toward a particularly interesting smell.

"No, keep walking pooch. I have to call Caitlin."

She glanced over her shoulder to be sure Paul wasn't watching her, then beeped the remote to open the doors, and boosted Sparky onto the seat. Tapping her phone, she waited for Caitlin to answer.

"Corporal Smith."

"Hey, it's me, Jessica."

"Sorry, I didn't look at the call display. What's up?" Caitlin asked.

"Do you have a minute?"

"Barely," she said, her terse tone was a little louder than the background voices.

"It sounds like you are at the station. I'll make this quick. I have found a security camera that might have recorded the back of the brewery."

"How?"

"Sparky and I went for a walk."

"Of course, you did. Why were you even looking?"

"You said that the brewery system malfunctioned and didn't record either the attack on Olivia or the one on Noah."

"Wait a second." Jessica listened as she heard Caitlin tell Ethan that she would be a moment, and then the background noises disappeared. "I did not tell you that. It's confidential information," Caitlin said, curtly.

"I know. I overheard you talking to Ethan about the security cameras and a problem with some of the footage. So, I scouted around the area and found a guy who has a camera that points in the direction of the brewery's back entrance."

A long heavy sigh echoed through Jessica's phone. "Please tell me you didn't ask for the video? That would screw up the chain of custody for the evidence."

"Nope. I have the guy's contact information. I'll text it to you. I told him my car was damaged, and I needed proof before the police could help me."

"You are annoying."

"Yep. But I did good, right?"

"I'll let you know." Caitlin disconnected.

"She hung up on me." Jessica looked at her phone, and then at Sparky. "She does that a lot." She sent Caitlin the information for Paul, the plumber, whose video doorbell overlooked the alley. "Let's go home and see what Mike is up to."

Chapter 42

Penticton RCMP station

Back at her desk, Caitlin studied the text message from Jessica, providing the first name, Paul, and a phone number for a nearby homeowner.

It might be nothing, but maybe the homeowner's security camera had caught something useful. Jessica was right. When they tried to review the footage from the back entrance, it jumped erratically forward. Even though the time stamp looked okay, something wasn't right with the recording.

"Evan, I have another job for you."

"What's up?" He pulled out a chair and sat down at her desk.

She handed him a slip of paper. "Call this guy ASAP for his address, and then go there. He might have CCTV footage of the alley behind the brewery. I need you to get a copy, and review it."

"How did you find him?"

"A confidential informant."

"Impressive. I didn't know you had a CI working with us on this case."

"Jessica."

"Got it," he grinned. "Sparky too?"

"Jessica phoned it in."

"I'm on it," he said.

The younger man's ability to dig out details made him a valuable member of their team. She hoped his shiny enthusiasm wouldn't tarnish too quickly with the daily grind of catching the bad guys, only to have them swiftly released by the courts.

Caitlin stood and surveyed the room. "Anyone know where Ethan is?"

Natalie's head popped up. "He got a phone call. He said he'd be back in about an hour."

"About this case?"

"Yes, he said the phone call was from Hayley VanBeck's mother."

"Okay, thanks." Caitlin rapidly typed a message to Ethan. *What are you doing?*

Hayley VB. Give me 20 min.

Okay.

Sergeant Williams suddenly appeared, and she involuntarily flinched.

"Sorry, I didn't mean to startle you," he said.

"No problem, Sarge. You walk so quietly that I didn't hear you."

"Kyla accuses me of deliberately sneaking up on her, but it's just the way I walk," he said.

"Do you like to dance?" she asked, while checking her phone for missed messages.

"Yes."

"That could explain it," she said, briefly making eye contact. "People who like to dance are usually light on their feet. They don't thump their feet when they walk."

With a tiny sardonic smile on his homely face, Williams said, "When we dance at Kyla's charity fundraisers, she says I'm her George Clooney."

Caitlin stifled a giggle.

"It's disrespectful for a subordinate to laugh at a superior officer," Williams said, the laughter in his eyes contradicting his reprimand.

"Noted sir," Caitlin responded. Her rebellious mouth twitched.

"Update me on your cases. The superintendent is breathing down my neck. She has given us twenty-four hours, and then SCU will take over."

"Only twenty-four hours?" Caitlin replied, dismayed. "Well, sleep is overrated." She moved to the whiteboard to summarize the various tasks that had been assigned, completed, and documented.

"Now, recap your current theories," Williams said.

"Sarah Wollman, the first death. By searching the CCTV, Evan has pinned down the arrival time of the four friends at the condo complex. Contrary to the statements from Olivia Caponera, Hayley VanBeck, and Noah Atkins, the principal renter Lucas Bankole, and one other unidentified male were home. They departed suddenly just ahead of the arrival of the ambulance crew. We are still trying to prove who spiked her drink, leading to her death," Caitlin said.

Williams silently motioned for her to continue.

"Olivia Caponera, case number two. Injured at Cactus Brewing when a tall stack of new beer cans, and several heavy pallets were pushed over onto her. Logan Wollman, the younger brother of Sarah Wollman, has admitted to his mother that he accidentally caused the incident. We are trying to confirm it was an accident, and not a deliberate attempt to hurt, or kill, Olivia."

She looked at Williams. "Any questions boss?"

"Keep going."

"Noah Atkins, case number three, and the second death. Ed Wollman, father of Sarah Wollman, has confessed to punching Noah Atkins, then thinking he was dead, panicked and hid the body in the kettle. We think that he had assistance from either his wife or his son. The other factor is Noah was not dead, he was unconscious. He drowned in the hot liquid."

Williams swallowed, hard. Thirty years as a cop, and he was still stunned by cold-hearted stupidity. "What can we do to wrap this up before tomorrow?"

"We need a break, boss," she said, as her phone rang. She lifted one finger, signaling Williams that she needed to answer the call. "It's Ethan. He left in a rush to meet with the VanBeck family."

Caitlin said to Ethan, "Tell me you have something good."

"I think I do," Ethan said. "Hayley VanBeck says she thinks Lucas Bankole put something in Sarah's drink. It was a special Christmas drink that he made for everyone, but also made sure that he personally handed a glass to each person."

"That's good. Now, we have to find Bankole. Anything else?" Caitlin asked.

"Hayley went to Olivia's home to check on her. Olivia told Hayley she was going to enlist Noah's help to create a podcast about her tragedy."

"A podcast just about her, and not her two deceased friends?"

"At the time, neither one had heard about Noah's death," Ethan said. "Hayley just found out and is terrified that she might be next. That's why she contacted me."

"So, does Hayley think that Lucas is responsible for these incidents?" Caitlin asked. "It seems a bit far-fetched."

"All I know is she's terrified of him. I think that's what prompted her to finally tell her mother about the party with Lucas and the other guy, Connor. Then her mother called me."

"Connor? Does she know his last name?"

"No. I have a vague description though. Older than her, maybe late 20s. Curly blonde hair and really pale skin. She said he looked Scandinavian."

"That's interesting, except I think Connor is more typically an Irish name," she said, then asked. "Are you on the way back?"

"Yep."

"Gotta go, Evan's calling," she said and disconnected the call. "Evan, have you got the video?"

"Yes! I had a quick look at the video. I think this is the break we need," he said. "I'll be there in ten minutes."

Williams waited until Caitlin ended her phone call, then raised one eyebrow in a question.

"I think we just caught a break, Sarge. Actually, two breaks. Ethan and Evan have two separate leads. They should both be here in a few minutes."

He gave her a thumbs up, and remained seated, waiting for the constables to return to the detachment.

Chapter 43

Penticton RCMP station

Sergeant Williams was still perched on the corner of a desk, waiting, when Evan and Ethan arrived within minutes of each other, flushed-faced, and excited about their finds.

"Evan has obtained a video from a homeowner's doorbell camera," Caitlin explained.

Williams nodded his eyes alive with interest.

Working at a nearby desk, Natalie joined the group.

Evan cued up the video, then said, "When I downloaded the video onto a USB, I checked the time setting on the homeowner's equipment to confirm that it was correct, and not still on daylight saving time. Keep your eyes on the back of the brewery. It happens quickly." He tapped play and moved aside.

Watching intently, Natalie was the first to speak. "Someone leaving in a rush. Wait, that's the Wollmans!"

"All three of the Wollmans," Caitlin said, as she noted the time. Then she turned to Williams to explain why she was excited about this new evidence. "It shows the Wollmans leaving by the back door of the brewery on the day that Noah died.

This is contrary to their previous statements," she said.

Williams indicated for her to continue.

"When Ed confessed to striking Noah and hiding his body in the kettle, Irene claimed she was too distraught to stop Ed. So, seeing her in this video isn't unexpected. But Irene also stated that Logan was out playing video games with friends, and now we know she was lying. Logan was at the brewery," Caitlin said.

"Ed could still be responsible for Noah's death, though," Natalie said.

"Maybe." Caitlin looked sharply at Natalie. "Think back to when you did the NOK for Sarah."

"It's hard to forget a death notification on Christmas morning," Natalie said.

"Did you notice Ed Wollman's hands?" Caitlin asked.

"No. Why?"

"When I interviewed him, he had healing cuts on three of his knuckles. It's been bothering me."

"Why? Sarah died on December 25th, and Noah died on December 27th. If Ed killed Noah, as he says he did, then his hands wouldn't have been injured when I did the NOK."

"I know. But, something about his injuries doesn't ring true."

"Did Dr. Liz find evidence of Noah being punched? Or was he hit with an object?" Ethan asked.

"Dammit. That's it! Dr. Liz gave me a verbal autopsy report. We haven't received the detailed report yet for Noah," she said. "Ethan, can you get on that right now?"

"Do you think Ed injured himself to make it look like he punched Noah?" Ethan asked.

Caitlin nodded. "That's where my thoughts are headed. We need the autopsy report to confirm how Noah was knocked out."

She sorted through the crime scene photos and found the one of a long wooden paddle, used in the brewing process. "Did this get fingerprinted? And if so, have we identified the prints?"

Evan checked a list. "The paddle was printed. No prints matched at the time. I'll get that rechecked now that we have prints from the three Wollmans."

"Absolutely," she agreed, "and as quickly as possible."

"Are we going to reinterview Irene?" Natalie asked.

"We'll reinterview both Irene and Logan, just as soon as we get that autopsy report," Caitlin said.

Ethan disconnected his call. "Dr. Liz is apologetic. Apparently, she intended to email her report yesterday, but she was interrupted and it was still sitting in her draft folder."

Both Caitlin and Ethan's phones pinged with an incoming message.

Ethan sat at the closest computer and logged in. He downloaded the document and then began to search for the cause of death. "Bingo, a large flat object was used to strike Noah on the back of his head. Similar to the wooden paddle. However, Dr. Liz couldn't find any trace evidence on it."

Frustrated Caitlin said, "Because Rhys used the paddle to pull out what he thought was a piece of cloth, contaminating the brew and washing away any trace evidence remaining on the paddle."

"Evan, anything on the fingerprints?"

"Not yet. It's only been a couple of minutes since I last checked."

"Where is Logan Wollman?" Sergeant Williams asked.

"After our interview with him last night, we reluctantly released him to his aunt, Tina Fellows," Caitlin said. "Both his mother and father have been booked into the remand center. We charged Logan with assault and endangering Olivia Caponera's life, but now I think we can link him to the murder of Noah Atkins."

"Does the aunt understand that she cannot take the boy away from Penticton?" Williams asked.

"She does. It was made very clear to her and to Logan's lawyer, Barry Kramer," Caitlin said.

"Anything else on the other two cases since your last update?" Williams asked.

Caitlin motioned to Ethan, and he said, "I have a witness, Hayley VanBeck, who thinks she saw Lucas Bankole spike Sarah Wollman's drink."

"Thinks?" Williams said.

"Hayley was at the same party, but somewhat occupied with another man, Connor, no last name.

When they first arrived, Lucas said he was making special Christmas drinks for everyone. Lucas had his back turned, but Hayley could see his hands hovering over the glass that he eventually handed to Sarah. And according to Hayley, when Sarah took a sip and set it aside, it was Lucas who insisted that she finish her drink," Ethan said.

"Between Hayley's statement and the security video, we can confirm that there were at least two adult men, plus the three young women, and Noah at that party," Evan said. "On the video, two men leave the building just minutes before the arrival of the ambulance."

"Can we get a decent snapshot from the video?" Caitlin asked. "To help us find this Connor guy."

Evan reached over onto his desk, "I meant to post this on the board earlier. It's a fairly good shot of both Lucas Bankole and his roommate Connor."

Studying the photo, Caitlin said to Evan, "I've been engrossed with Noah's death and forgot to ask if you found anything more about the two construction companies that Bankole or Fortier used as a reference?"

"I did an extensive search," Evan replied. "Neither one exists. The references were bogus."

"Mr. Morgan said he spoke to the owners of both the construction companies. According to him, both men said Louis Fortier, who we know as Lucas Bankole, was a terrific employee. Dependable. Reliable," Caitlin said.

"I know. I have searched everywhere and neither of those companies exist. I think Bankole used other friends to fake the references," Evan responded.

"That's not surprising, given what we know about him now," Ethan said.

An incoming message dinged on Evan's phone.

"It's a match for Logan's fingerprints," Evan said. "The techs found a partial print on the forklift steering wheel and a single print on the access hatch of the kettle. Both match to Logan's prints."

"Yes!" Caitlin shouted, then turned to Ethan. "We need a search warrant for the Wollman's home and vehicles."

"On it."

"Great work team," Williams said. "I knew you could do it."

"Thanks, boss. We still have a lot of details to wrap up, but I am confident that we've solved the attack on Olivia Caponera, and the death of Noah Atkins."

"And Sarah Wollman's death?" Williams asked.

"We know what happened, but we don't know where Lucas Bankole is at the moment," Caitlin replied. "We'll keep on it."

Chapter 44

The Naramata cottage

"And here I am celebrating New Year's Eve with my date, Sparky," Caitlin said as she rubbed Sparky's tummy.

Cuddled on the sofa with Mike, Jessica stared sleepily into the fire. "Did the CCTV footage that I located help solve your murder case?" she asked.

Caitlin sighed and rolled into an upright position. For some reason, she found it harder to answer questions while sprawled on the comfortable loveseat. "Yes, it gave us enough evidence to charge the Wollmans."

"All three of them?" Mike asked. "Even their son, Logan?"

"Yes, all three are waiting for their separate trial dates. Ed Wollman and Irene Wollman have been charged with aiding and abetting, because they helped Logan cover up the attacks on both Olivia Caponera and Noah Atkins. We have also charged Logan with the murder of Noah Atkins, although his parents are still maintaining that Ed was responsible and not their son."

"God, that's sad," Jessica said.

"It's tragic," Caitlin said. "As for Olivia Caponera, she has given up on her dream to get rich with a podcast about her ordeal. Instead, she's hiding at home, refusing to return to work at the brewery. I have suggested to her mother that Olivia needs counseling. I think she has a form of PTSD."

"What about the other families?"

"Hayley VanBeck's parents have put their family home up for sale. They plan to move their daughter to a different city, far away from Olivia, in hopes of giving her a more stable life, away from wild parties, drugs, and older men," Caitlin made a face, "I'm not sure it will work. She is legal age, and has a taste for guys who are about ten years older."

"I guess they have to do what they think is best for their daughter," Mike said.

"Umm."

"And Noah's parents?" Jessica asked.

"George and Laura Atkins are staying in their home. They have many close friends who have rallied around them, providing emotional support...and endless casseroles," she said, with a slight smile. "I stopped by to check on them. Laura invited me in for a cup of tea and then opened the refrigerator door to display the many casseroles stacked inside. They won't need to shop for a while."

"It's good to have caring neighbors when your world falls apart," Mike said.

"The sad thing is, if Sarah had stayed home on Christmas Eve like she wanted to, none of this would have happened. It is a terrible tragedy for everyone," Caitlin said.

"It's heartbreaking," Jessica agreed. "Did you ever find the two guys who live in the condo?"

"Not yet," Caitlin replied. "Lucas Bankole now has two active Canada-wide warrants for his arrest, one for a previous charge of drug trafficking and the second one because he is wanted for questioning about Sarah Wollman's death. And his roommate, Connor is also a person of interest in Sarah's death but we still don't know his last name."

"Are they still paying rent?"

"No. They are long gone."

"So, Sarah Wollman's case is unresolved?" Mike asked.

"For now," Caitlin said. "But I'm confident we will apprehend our suspect. The Mounties always get their man."

What she couldn't divulge to Mike and Jessica, was the unconfirmed rumors that a rival drug dealer and two of his buddies had attacked a man matching Lucas' description. Unable to prove or disprove the story, she had fruitlessly checked the local hospitals. If the story was true, he might have survived and fled the area, or he might have been killed and dumped on a secluded mountain trail.

Either way, she would continue searching for him, or his remains. She wanted justice for Sarah Wollman.

Chapter 45

The Naramata cottage

In the kitchen, Jessica cradled a hot cup of coffee in her hands, contemplating sneaking back into their bedroom for a warmer pair of socks. Buried under the warm comforter, Mike was still dozing, and she didn't want to wake him, but the tiled floors were uncomfortably chilly.

Their New Year's Eve dinner with Caitlin had ended around ten the night before. Reluctant to leave her vindictive cat alone, Caitlin had switched to drinking soda water for the last couple of hours. Tickle the Terrible liked to shred Caitlin's slippers if she was feeling lonely and abandoned.

Jessica looked toward their bedroom. *Get my socks? Or wait for Mike to wake up?*

The Okanagan winter hadn't been the bone-chilling cold of the previous two years, but it wasn't Mexico-warm either. The nine days she'd been on Isla Mujeres had reset her temperature tolerance range from Canadian, back to Caribbean.

She heard Mike moving around in the bedroom, then he called, "Good morning, sunshine."

"Morning, honey. Would you like a cup of coffee?" She asked, raising her voice a little.

"Yes, please!"

She heard the toilet flush, and a moment later Mike sauntered toward her, smiling. Her eyes roamed his naked body. "Mmm, nice view, but aren't you cold?" She set her cup on the counter and stepped toward him, wrapping her arms around his body and placing her warm hands firmly on his butt.

"I was." He kissed her deeply. "But that warmed me up nicely."

"Your coffee will be another minute or two."

"Okay, I'll get dressed," he said strolling back to the bedroom.

Admiring his body as he walked away, she foamed the hot milk and poured it into a tall mug of strong coffee.

Mike returned buttoning his shirt, and kissed her again. "What's on your agenda today?"

"Not much. Do you need help at either of the wineries?" She asked, referring to *On the Edge*, where they lived and worked, and *No Regrets* where Mike was still the consulting winemaker.

Mike rubbed a hand over his smooth head and mentally ran through his list. "I don't need help, but if you and Sparky want to hang out with me today while I check on a few things, I'd love your company." Sitting at the table, he scrolled through his phone, checking for winery-related emails. *Nothing urgent.*

Jessica sat beside him. Tucking her chin against one shoulder, she studied his profile and said, "Yes."

Distracted by an email from another winery owner, Mike replied, "So, you and Sparky will come with me?"

"Yes, to your other question," she replied, waiting to see if he would make the connection.

He slowly set his phone on the table and searched her face. "Are you teasing me?"

"I'm not teasing. My answer is yes."

With a whoop, he jumped up and pulled Jessica to her feet. "Jessica Sanderson, are you saying you'll marry me?"

"Of course. What did you think I was saying yes to?"

"Finally!"

Laughing Jessica kissed him. "I love you, Mike Lyons. Completely."

"And I love you! Let's get married as soon as possible."

Putting one hand on his chest, she pushed him back a few inches. "Slow down. What's the rush."

"I want to get married before you change your mind."

"I won't change my mind."

"You might." He reached for a calendar, one of the old-style paper ones given out by real estate companies in time for the new year. "How about this coming Saturday? It would be a great day to get married," he said, pressing his index finger on the date as if he was preventing it from disappearing.

"Mike, we have family. Mom, Dad, and my brothers can drive from the coast and be here in five to six hours, but your parents have to fly in from Ontario. It's too much of a rush."

"I can book their flights. Right now."

Jessica broke from his embrace, and gently pushed down on his shoulder, "Stop. Sit. Take a breath."

He slowly sunk onto a chair, still holding her hand. "I have been so damn scared that you were going to say no," he said.

"I'm so sorry that I left you hanging," she said, laying her palm on his face. "I was afraid we would screw up our fantastic romance with marriage."

"What changed your mind?"

"I don't want to spend my life with anyone but you, and if being married is important to you, then let's get married," she said. "But you have to make an unbreakable promise."

"Anything."

"I want to keep laughing and dancing with you. Anytime. Anyplace. In the kitchen. On the deck. On a beach. Or in the streets of Paris. Anywhere. You promise?"

"I promise." He stood and pulled her close, then started swaying back and forth. "Even without music, I love dancing with you," he said, then stopped abruptly, "Is this okay or does your toe still hurt?"

"My toe is fine, unless you feel the need to break some moves."

"Nope. This is good," he said. "So, this Saturday?"

"April 1st," she countered.

"You want to get married on April Fool's Day?"

"Yep, so that we remember to have fun, and don't take ourselves too seriously."

Mike sighed. "You win. I'll happily be your April Fool."

Smiling at him, she picked up her unfinished coffee and dumped it down the sink. "I'm going to Facetime my parents. And you should call yours."

Tapping her phone, she called her mother, "Hi, Mom."

"Hi, sweetie." Her mother's face smiled back at her.

"Remember you said you would like to come to the valley to do some wine tasting?"

"Yes, I remember," Anne Sanderson replied.

"Mike and I are getting married, on April 1st. Mark it on your calendar."

Chapter 46

Cactus Brewing

Three months later, the brewery buzzed with activity. It had been a long shut-down while the family reequipped the brewery and rebuilt customer confidence.

A new kettle arrived in February. The pipe fitters had installed it and replaced all of the lines leading to the fermentation tanks. Pumps, filters, lines, anything that could have been contaminated by the incident in December had been replaced.

A strong marketing campaign, including progress photos to reassure the public that the situation was being handled, had helped to build excitement.

The reopening on April 11th would coincide with the start of the annual Okanagan Fest of Ale.

The End

I hope you enjoyed this story! Like every self-published writer, I rely heavily on recommendations and reviews to sell my books. If you enjoyed reading this book, or any of my *Isla Mujeres Mysteries* or the *Death in the Vineyards* mysteries, please leave a review. Tell your friends, tell your family, or anyone who will listen. Word-of-mouth is enormously helpful. Thank you!

Thank you!

I would like to extend my thanks to the entire team at Cannery Brewing in Penticton for being a great source of information and for assisting with explanations of the brewing process and terminology used in this book. Thanks to Patt, Ron, Ian, Ross, Max and Kim for their support and extra guidance.

While this book is not based on Cannery Brewing, there are some similarities that some Cannery fans may recognize. Cannery Brewing was one of the first craft breweries in Penticton. They brewed their first batch of beer, their signature Naramata Nut Brown Ale, on April Fool's Day, 2001. In the beginning, they brewed and sold beer out of their brewery in the historic Cannery Trade Centre, in an old Alymer Fruit and Vegetable cannery.

In 2015, Cannery Brewing built a new purpose-built brewery on Ellis Street in beautiful downtown Penticton. Their family-friendly taproom, patio and seasonal backyard are worth a visit when visiting Penticton. They feature a selection of their own handcrafted beers, local

Canned by Lynda L. Lock

BC wines and cider, an offering of delicious dishes and sharing plates, and a robust events schedule.

A bit about the author:

Steve Emshay, Richard Grierson, Lynda Lock, Dave Prechel (Back) Lawrie Lock, and his sister Linda Grierson

Co-owner of the 1ˢᵗ South Okanagan craft brewery, *Tin Whistle Brewing Co*.

It began with a phone call between Lawrie Lock, and his sister Linda Grierson. In 1994, Linda and her husband Richard, suggested that the four of us open the first craft brewery in the south Okanagan. It took a year to buy a property, remodel it, order custom-made tanks and equipment, and more importantly learn how to make English-style ales.

We opened the *Tin Whistle Brewing Company* in August 1995 with three ales; Penticton Pale Ale, Whistle Stop Dark, and Rattlesnake ESB. Three months later we changed the names to Coyote Pale, Black Widow Dark, and kept Rattlesnake ESB. By 1996 we had added Peaches and Cream, and Killer Bee Dark Honey.

In 1998, local businesswoman, Lorraine Nagy, approached us, asking if we were interested in selling our company. Yes, we were! We had enjoyed the challenge of the startup and were ready for a new adventure.

Lorraine Nagy remained the owner of *Tin Whistle* until 2021, when she sold it to the current owners, Alexis Esseltine, Tim Scoon, and their family.

The legal stuff

Canned
Published by Lynda L. Lock
Copyright 2025
Electronic Book: ISBN 978-1-738-3955-2-1
Paperback: ISBN 978-1-738-3955-3-8
Hardcover: ISBN 978-1-738-3955-4-5

Acknowledgments

Writing is a solitary obsession with hours spent creating, considering, and correcting.

However, I have had assistance from some amazing people:

- Captain Tony Garcia for the beautiful cover photos for the first three novels. Both Tony and Betsy Snider are valuable sources of information about island life.
- Carmen Amato, mystery writer and creator of the Emilia Cruz Detective Series, re-designed my original attempt at designing a book cover.
- Good friends Diego Medina and Jeff McGahee who patiently tweaked the cover for *Tormenta Isla* until I was happy with the results.
- Diego Medina created the covers for *Temptation Isla, Terror Isla*, and *Twisted Isla*.
- Mary Fry Designs created the cover of *Corked, Smashed, Crushed*, *Canned,* and *Tangled Isla*.
- Patricio Yam Dzul, Freddy Medina, and Eva Velázquez are cherished friends who are always willing to share their life stories.
- My treasured group of manuscript proofreaders include Sue Lo, Janice Carlisle Rodgers, Kyla Daman-Willems, Kim Lawton, and John Arendt. I truly appreciate your helpful suggestions and corrections; any and all remaining errors are my responsibility.

You can also follow Sparky and me on social media:
- Notes from Paradise, A Writer's Life_on blogspot
- Facebook @ Lynda L Lock Author's Page
- Instagram @lyndalockauthor
- Amazon @ Lynda L Lock
- Bookbub @ Lynda L Lock
- Goodreads @ Lynda L Lock

Like this book?
Try the others.

Treasure Isla Book #1

Treasure Isla is a humorous Caribbean adventure set on Isla Mujeres, a tiny island off the eastern coast of Mexico. Two twenty-something women find themselves in possession of a seemingly authentic treasure map, which leads them on a chaotic search for buried treasure while navigating the dangers of too much tequila, disreputable men, and a killer. And there is a dog, a lovable rescue mutt named Sparky.

Trouble Isla Book #2

"This pair of leading ladies are fun to immerse in for an afternoon escape. The character development is richly layered and entertaining. The stakes are also enjoyably high, and the action sequences will keep readers voraciously flipping pages. Trouble Isla is a quick, unpredictable read. Bringing this small Caribbean island to life, and populating it with vivid characters that will continue to carry this series forward, Lynda L. Lock has created a uniquely colorful mystery." Self-Publishing Review, ★★★★

Tormenta Isla Book #3

A mysterious disappearance of a local man and the looming threat of multiple hurricanes headed toward the peaceful Caribbean island of Isla Mujeres creates havoc in the lives of Jessica, her friends, and her rescue mutt, Sparky.

Diego held up his smartphone and silently showed her the screen, pointing at the NOAA graphics.

Her eyes opened wide in surprise as she looked at the screen, then a frown crinkled her brow. "Really? Three hurricanes?"

"*Si*," he responded, "Pablo, Rebekah, y Sebastien."

Temptation Isla Book #4

Rafael Fernandez leaned forward resting his elbows on the polished wood, tapping his finger-tips together. "Take them all out! At the reception."

"As you wish, Don Rafael." Alfonso Fuentes' jaw muscle twitched with tension.

"You don't agree?" Fernandez snarled.

Alfonso paused momentarily considering his next words. He had to get this exactly right or he would, at the very least, be demoted to the riskiest tasks or in the worse-case scenario killed for insubordination. Depending on Fernandez's mood, the flick of a finger or a chin pointed at a victim could quickly end that person's life.

Terror Isla Book #5

Isla Mujeres, a tiny island paradise in the Caribbean Sea, is rocked by a power struggle between a Mexican cartel and a Romanian gang as they battle for control of the illegitimate ATM skimming. Big changes are coming for Carlos and Yasmin, while Jessica Sanderson fends off an angry lover from her past. Sparky, Jessica's stocky beach mutt, is once again at the center of another Sparky-situation.

"I want a super-hero cape. A red one," Diego Avalos said. "I am feeling very underappreciated."

"In Jessica's opinion, Sparky is the super-hero with the red cape. We're just his minions doing his bidding," Pedro rejoined.

Who's going to save who? Join the adventure to find out.

Twisted Isla Book #6

Death stalks the annual Island Time Music Festival. Nashville musicians and songwriters flock to the tropical island of Isla Mujeres to raise funds for the Little Yellow School House. Jessica and her keen-nosed beach-mutt Sparky are thrown into another murder mystery.

Sergeant Ramirez held up his palm with his fingers spread wide, "That's the fifth."

"Fifth what?" Asked Mike Lyons.

"Body," answered Ramirez, his eyes sweeping to Jessica's face. "That we've had to question señorita Sanderson about."

"Really?" Mike lobbed a startled look at Jessica.

Tangled Isla Book #7

Has an unidentified killer of several Florida women relocated to the tropical paradise of Isla Mujeres?

Leading up to the busiest time of the year on Isla Mujeres, four young women, similar in appearance to the Florida victims, are unaccounted for and have been reported as missing by concerned friends.

Longing for a reunion with her island friends, Jessica Sanderson returns to Mexico on a solo visit, leaving her partner Mike Lyons with the challenging task of babysitting her legendary and finicky dog, Sparky.

When Jessica arrives on the island, she is persuaded to participate in the annual children's parade, wearing the Minnie Mouse costume. The parade is disrupted by an unexplained event, and becomes entangled in the mystery of the missing women.

Will Jessica be able to solve this mystery without the help of Sparky, her famous clue-finding pooch?

CORKED Book #1 Death in the Vineyards

Love, lust, and loot in the affluent world of wine and wineries.

Corked is the newest murder mystery from the author of the exciting Isla Mujeres Mysteries. Murder follows Jessica Sanderson and her detective dog Sparky as they relocate from their Caribbean paradise in Mexico to the Okanagan wine country in Canada. On Isla Mujeres, big changes are coming for Jessica's friends as the COVID-19 virus gains momentum. Leaving her beloved island, Jessica follows her new love interest, Mike Lyons, into a new adventure.

SMASHED Book #2 Death in the Vineyards

Some people can convince themselves they can do no wrong.

While wildfires ravage the Okanagan Valley, Jessica Sanderson and her love interest Mike Lyons battle to save two wineries; one from the massive wildfire that is threatening homes and businesses in Okanagan Falls, and the other from economic disaster and the sudden death of their winemaker.

In *Smashed*, Jessica and her Mexi-mutt Sparky find themselves in the middle of a sticky situation. In this highly-anticipated sequel to *Corked*, inquisitive Jessica and the amazing nose of Sparky are once again caught up in a police investigation.

CRUSHED Book #3 Death in the Vineyards

Tragedy strikes from a clear blue sky.

While creating a new life for themselves in the Okanagan Valley's wine region, Jessica Sanderson and Mike Lyons become entangled in another unexpected death.

Crushed takes us on a wild ride of intertwined tragedies, family secrets, and substance abuse, while RCMP Corporal Caitlin Smith races to solve the murder and unravel the surrounding mystery.

www.ingramcontent.com/pod-product-compliance
Lightning Source LLC
Chambersburg PA
CBHW070636260626
47161CB00007B/2725